DEL RYDER AND THE
CRYSTAL SEED

Matthew David Brough

DEL RYDER AND THE CRYSTAL SEED

Matthew David Brough

Background image from www.Shutterstock.com
Cover design by Roseanna White Designs,
www.RoseannaWhiteDesigns.com

To my mum who taught me to pretend.
To my daughter who reminds me to play.
And to my wife who stands beside me at every step.

CHAPTER ONE

The Glass and the Tombstone

Del Ryder, partially hidden by a large tree trunk, was about to witness a stand off. Guy Thomkins inched his large frame along the wall of the old stone church, his weapon held at attention next to his head, ready to take aim at his enemy. He quickly knelt to the ground, and rather than peeking around the corner, he rolled out into the open in an attempt to throw off his opponent. He lifted his arms, and then it was all noise.

"Bang."

"Bang, bang, bang."

"You're dead! I got you!" Guy announced.

"I'm totally not," Phil yelled back. "You didn't hit me, not even close."

"It's always the same with you two," Del said, coming out from her hiding place. "You can't play a game of guns without arguing about who got hit first."

She tossed her bent piece of wood, which doubled as her weapon, to the ground.

"I'm sick of this game anyway," she continued. "We should have played swords. It's way harder to argue about who gets hit in swords."

"But swords hurts more." Sam Long, the youngest and smallest of the group, rounded the corner of the church from where Guy had come. Sam always voted for guns over swords, proving to his three best friends that they were right in claiming that he was the wimp of the bunch.

"Let's just start again," said Phil.

Phil Coons, almost thirteen, and the oldest by a month over Guy, made most of the decisions for the four friends. They all knew that his words were less suggestion and more command.

"Twenty seconds. Go!"

They each counted to twenty out loud as they scattered.

Del jumped a fence, but on getting clear of the hedge that ran along the south side of the cemetery, she spotted the dark figure of a man coming out of the ancient church.

It was the priest. They had run from him many times before. There was always a risk of bumping into him, but the churchyard was simply the best place to play guns, so they always returned to this spot. As the priest's head turned in Del's direction, she dove back toward the hedge, sliding under a sparse section. She was pretty sure he hadn't seen her.

*****

Del, facedown, felt a cold smooth gravestone beneath her. She wasn't thrilled with the idea of lying on top of it, but she dared not move either, not knowing the location of the priest. As her eyes adjusted to the dim light under the hedge, she could make out an old inscription on the stone. She read at the top "BLYTHE" and underneath it "1875 - 1889." Unable to stop her mind from doing the math, Del knew in less than a second that whoever Blythe was, he had died at age fourteen. If she wasn't creeped out enough lying on top of someone's grave, now it was worse. He was a kid like her when he died, just three years her senior. Del couldn't conceive of her life ending that early.

She looked up a little and tried to see where the priest might be. She couldn't see or hear anyone. Most likely Phil, Guy, and Sam had seen the priest as well and were laying low in one of their usual spots. She hadn't had time to get to where they usually hid, but this place was even better. Not even Sam would find her there and Sam always found the best hiding spots.

As she edged forward, attempting to look beyond the hedge, out of the corner of her eye, she noticed what looked like a small piece of bottle-green glass embedded in the ground beside Blythe's stone. Del reached for the object with two fingers. As soon as she made contact with the glass, it flashed with a deep glowing light. She quickly pulled her hand away, shocked. The glow disappeared. Tentatively, Del brought her hand back over the glass. She touched it again, and the same deep flash of light appeared.

What was that? How could a piece of glass light up like that? Even without a piece of magic glass, Del would have wanted to show her friends this hiding spot. She was determined to find them and bring them back to the gravestone and the glass.

Crouching, she parted a few of the branches and looked out from her cover. There was no sign of the priest, so she crawled out from under the hedge and headed into the churchyard toward the place where the boys were most likely to have hidden.

*****

Del approached the edge of a small treed area of the churchyard where there sat an old rundown shed that she and her friends loved hiding in for their game of guns. There were spy holes on every side, and one hole in the padlocked door that was large enough to squeeze through. The shed was full of rusty paint cans and other containers filled with chemicals and old, solidified substances that were once liquid. It's a wonder they didn't make themselves sick from inhaling the fumes inside that place, and it's a wonder the thing didn't spontaneously go up in flames.

"Phil? Guy?" Del paused, listening. "Sam?"

Sunlight was fading fast as dusk approached. An eerie mist had rolled in making it difficult to see much beyond the tree line behind the padlocked fire hazard. Everything was silent. No one was shooting their imaginary bullets at her. No one was yelling. There were no whispered or muffled arguments about who had hit whom in the game.

Maybe her friends couldn't see her with all the weird fog. Maybe they had been caught by the priest.

Del crept closer to the shed, and peered through one of the holes. Total darkness met her eyes.

"Guys? Are you in there?" she whispered. "If you're in there, this isn't funny."

Her friends loved playing practical jokes on Del. They had gotten her so many times. She always played along, getting mad at them in a way that showed that she liked the attention. Only Sam ever seemed to pick up that deep down she didn't actually like it. That was the real truth. Del didn't like being picked on or made fun of, even if it did make her one of the guys.

"Guys! Seriously!" Del's voice was starting to raise above a whisper. She crept around the back of the shed and tried, unsuccessfully, to see into the small forest.

"Phil - are you there?"

Maybe they had gone home. And where was the priest? Was he hunting them? Had he found her friends? She didn't know if she should leave or not. It was getting dark, and her mom would expect her home really soon.

She squinted into the foggy dusk of the forest and thought she saw the black shape of a man. She stayed silent and still. If it was the priest, she was pretty sure he hadn't seen her. She backed up slowly, keeping her eye on her potential assailant.

Suddenly a hand arched across the top part of her chest, just under her neck, grabbing her shoulder. Del nearly jumped out of her skin, but before she could scream, her attacker's other hand covered her mouth.

*****

"Shh," said her attacker.

Del wriggled trying to get free but he had a good grip on her. A series of ideas raced through her head, as she tried to think of how she could escape. Stomp on his foot. Elbow to the stomach. Poke at his eyes. She tried to twist away, but to no avail. She kept screaming all the time, but his hand acted as an excellent muffler.

"Shh," he commanded again. "Del, be quiet. It's me. It's Guy. You've gotta be quiet. The priest is out there."

Del relaxed a little, and Guy loosened his grip. She whipped around, punched him in the gut, and whispered "I know he's out there; I could see him. What're you doing grabbing me like that!"

Guy looked down and shuffled his feet. Del noticed Phil lurking near the corner of the shed with the usual smirk he wore when the joke was on Del. It was obvious that Guy was just doing as Phil had ordered. His loyalty to Phil was absolutely unwavering, but it was clear that he didn't always like the antics Phil made him get up to when it involved Del. Guy liked her - not as much as he liked other girls, but he liked her.

Del walked over to Phil and punched him in the arm. "Where's Sam?" she asked.

"Don't know," Phil replied. "We haven't seen him since we took off. Maybe the priest got him."

"I thought maybe the priest had gotten all of you," said Del. "But I just saw him walking in the woods. Sam's got to be hiding. We've got to find him, 'cause I need to show you guys something."

The three of them set off, away from the woods and the shed, back a little bit toward the church. They were hesitant to call out too loudly, but as it got darker, their voices increased in volume, as they kept calling his name.

"Let's just go home," said Phil. "Sam probably just went home."

Del knew that there was no way Sam would leave without them. She also knew Sam would be a little bit scared to walk home in this fog and a lot scared hiding on his own with the priest wandering around. She imagined him curled up in a shivering ball almost crying, waiting for his friends to pass by so that he could rub his eyes and bounce out once he was sure that there were no tears coming. It wasn't just that Sam was only ten years old. He was sensitive and was not good at acting tough, like Del. Sam was sometimes scared to show his sensitive side to Phil and Guy, but Del had seen it a few times before.

Phil, Guy, and Del arrived at the corner of the church and without thinking rounded the corner. There before them was their nemesis.

*****

"Hello there," said the priest, smiling.

All three of them took off, taking the most direct route to the lane. Sam came flying out of a nearby bush and joined the sprint-retreat. Del looked over her shoulder and saw the priest in exactly the place they left him, with the same smile on his face, now shaking his head.

Phil and Guy had no regard for the slower Del and Sam. They just ran. Del's house was only about a 5 minute run from the church along Farmer road. Phil had the side gate open in time for Guy and then the other two to come flying in to the safety of the yard.

"That was awesome," said Guy.

"That was close," said Phil.

"Too close," said Sam.

Del was anxious to tell her story about the glass. "You guys, I found something. Something really cool."

"Whatever it is, it's probably lame," said Phil.

"It's totally not!" said Del.

"C'mon, Deli," said Phil, using the nickname Del wouldn't let on that she hated. "You always think you have the coolest thing to say, and it's always something dumb."

"Let her talk already." Sam trailed off as he spoke, aware that his status in their foursome did not merit such a challenge to Phil's leadership.

But Sam so rarely stood up to Phil that, this time, he let him get away with it. The three boys fell silent as Del began to tell them about everything she had found: the great hiding place under the hedge, the gravestone, and most importantly, the glowing glass.

At the mention of the light in the glass, Phil objected. "As if that happened! It was probably just the sun hitting it or something."

"Then let's go back tomorrow," Del said. "You can see for yourselves."

"It just sounds like there is a dumb piece of bottle stuck in the ground," said Phil.

He wasn't buying her story, but Del knew what she had seen, and she hoped it would be there when they went back.

Phil continued, "I guess we can go back tomorrow and look, but just to prove that you're crazy."

Sam and Guy agreed, and as they did, Del sensed they both wanted to see what she had seen.

"You kids want a snack?" Del's mom stood in the frame of the door with some lemonade and a box of cookies.

Del rolled her eyes at the suggestion, and at her mother's perfectly done makeup and the ridiculous outfit she was wearing. She desperately wished she would act like a regular mom instead of trying to relive her lost college years or whatever.

"No thanks Mrs. Ryder." Phil put on his nicest *I'm talking to a parent voice*. "I need to be getting home for supper."

"You can all call me Amy."

"You better stay away from calling her Mrs. Ryder too." Del's rolling eyes turned to daggers. "She's Ms. Stevens now."

The divorce had happened when Del was eight years old, but Del's mom had only just recently gone back to her old name. The name change coincided with her sudden shift in fashion and her obsession with perfect hair and nails. Del was sick of hearing her Mom talk about how she was finally putting herself "out there."

"Sorry," Phil said. "I forgot."

"That's fine. Anyway - I'm Amy to you boys."

"Okay, uh… Amy." Guy chimed in, doing something weird with his voice trying to make it somehow sound lower than it was. "I, uh, need to be going as well."

At that, Del pushed Phil, Guy, and Sam out the gate and slammed it behind them.

"See you tomorrow morning at the place? Nine o'clock?" Sam called.

"Yeah. I guess so." Del was way more excited about going back to the churchyard than her tone suggested.

*****

Del headed into the house to find that the lemonade and cookies were the extent of the plan for supper.

"I'm going out tonight," her mom said. "Suzanne is watching you. She'll make you some food."

"I don't need my sister to watch me," Del

complained. "And I don't know what you think happens when you're not around. I'll be the one making food for her and probably her boyfriend, too."

"No, no, sweetheart. Suzanne and I had a chat - you're going to have a great girls' night. Friday night sisters' night! She said she's going to pick out a girl's movie for you two to watch together."

"As if that's going to happen."

Del's Friday nights for the last three months had consisted of her mother going out and her acting as babysitter to her older sister and her sister's boyfriend, Jack. Del had given him the oh-so-clever nickname Jerk, but was too frightened to ever call him that to his face. On Fridays, Del was always the one to make sure Suzanne and Jerk had some supper and didn't mess up the house too much, or burn it down. There was that one time that Jerk wanted to light some candles for the "romance." The two of them left the candles unattended while they went to the store to get some candy, and the curtain almost went up in smoke. Del, fortunately, had found the candles before anything terrible happened. She never told her mom about the incident; nor any of the other incidents, her secrecy enforced by Jerk's threats, and, in that one case, a small share in the candy.

Jerk came over about an hour after Del's mom had left. Del had already whipped up some scrambled eggs and toast for them to eat.

"These eggs are terrible," said Jerk, after grabbing them for himself. "They're totally cold."

"I cooked them twenty minutes ago," said Del, "Those are just our leftovers. I didn't know you would want any."

"Why don't you make some new ones?" Jerk ordered.

"Sorry JACK." Del made sure to not call him Jerk. "Those were the last eggs."

"Maybe you should go to the store and get some more, then."

"I'm only eleven, and I'm not allowed to go to the store by myself after dark. Maybe you should order a pizza."

"You're lippy tonight," said Jerk. "What's wrong with you? Usually you're up in your room crying by now. Off you go now. I need some time with my babe."

"She's just growing up - aren't you Deli," said Suzanne. "She's got three boyfriends, y'know. That Guy guy is kind of cute. Maybe you should settle on just him. But I guess if you can have three boyfriends, why not?"

Jerk rolled his eyes as Del punched her sister in the arm.

"Shut up, Suzanne," Del said.

"I heard you talking about some stupid thing you found at the church," said Suzanne, changing the subject. "Jack, you know our little Deli's found religion down at the old church. Be careful with those three boyfriends, though - I'm pretty sure God looks down on that kind of thing."

Del, at age eleven, was intelligent well beyond her years, but she always had trouble outdoing the insults that her teenage sister could come up with. This was why Jerk was basically right; she spent most of her Friday nights upstairs in tears. They were almost always tears of frustration. Frustration at her life, frustration at being confused about her relationship with her mom, frustration at having to grow up too fast, and frustration at not being able to fight back against her sister and Jerk. The tears started to well up.

"Oh. Here they come. Time for the waterworks." Jerk was relentless.

"Seriously, Deli." Suzanne tried to pull things back a bit. "What did you find out there?"

"Nothing! Nothing! And even if there was something out there, you're the last people I would tell." Del stormed upstairs.

"So, you don't mind if we come with you out there in the morning?" Suzanne called.

Del made it to her room before she started to seriously break down. She slammed the door and buried her face in her pillow. What should have been a night of excited anticipation at whatever discovery they would make the next day turned into a tear-soaked pillowcase. Del couldn't stop her mind from spinning in circles for what seemed like hours. Finally, her thoughts fell on, of all things, Sam. Somehow just picturing her best friend calmed her down. She thought about texting him but unexpectedly felt kind of nervous about it.

Her phone vibrated in her hand. The message just said "can't wait for tomorrow." It was Sam. Del finally got that bit of excitement back in her gut: just enough to strike the right balance to lead to a good night's sleep. Maybe with her friends by her side in the morning, all would be well.

CHAPTER TWO

Digging Out a Door

Del did not need the alarm she had set for herself. She was up and ready to go by seven, two hours before she was supposed to meet the boys. She was worried that her sister would follow through on the threat she had made the night before to join Del in the churchyard. Del knew teenage Suzanne loved her sleep far more than any threats she might make to spoil Del's fun, but even so, Del had decided to be careful.

Del sat just outside Suzanne's room listening and looking intently for any sign of movement. She slowly ate a bowl of Captain Crunch and sipped some apple juice. By the time she was finished her early breakfast, she still had an hour and a half to wait until she could safely slip away, assured that her sister wouldn't show up at the churchyard. While there was a slight chance that Suzanne might wake up early, there was absolutely no chance Jerk would. He had likely gone home after one o'clock in the morning, and there was no way he would be moving before noon.

After half an hour of waiting, Del couldn't take it.

She wasn't sure why she was so nervous about her sister. Perhaps she somehow sensed the magnitude of what was going to happen that day to her and her three "boyfriends," and she just didn't want her sister to have any part in it. The more Del tried to think of other things, the more she worried about her sister waking. Then it hit her between the eyes. What if she had set an alarm?

Del reached for the doorknob, turned it, and opened the door into her sister's room. It squeaked, and Suzanne turned over. Del froze. Without further movement from the teenager, Del proceeded toward the bedside table. No alarm was set on Suzanne's antique clock-radio. Del turned to go back into the hall, a little relieved, and then saw her sister's phone lying on the floor plugged into the wall. She grabbed it and quickly realized an alarm was set. One problem - she didn't know her sister's passcode to get into the phone and turn it off. She could flip the vibrate switch so the phone wouldn't make any other sound than a hum, but that would likely be enough to wake Suzy light-sleeper. She could think of two options: flip the phone to vibrate and cover it with something to muffle the sound, or unplug the phone and take it downstairs. Either way her sister would flip, but Del knew if she removed the alarm her sister would stay in bed until at least eleven, maybe noon. She decided to take the phone downstairs. Better safe than sorry, and if she was already going to be in trouble, she figured she had better make sure there was no chance Suzanne was going to hear it.

Del took the phone downstairs, then scrambled back up to sit in the hall and wait. At eight forty-five, she decided it was time to get moving. She snuck down the stairs, and as she left through the back door, she could hear the gentle hum of the phone on the carpeted living room floor.

*****

Del arrived at the edge of the churchyard five minutes early, and to her surprise, Phil, Guy, and Sam were already there.

"What kept you?" Guy said. "You ready to show us the lame glass or what?"

Phil interjected: "Hold on a sec. Before we do anything, we need to check for the priest or anyone else who might be around."

This was unusually cautious for Phil, but this morning, he was somehow much more aware than usual. He was in leader mode. He got like this occasionally. No joking, no nonsense. This was Phil Coons at his best. Phil led them in a kind of zig zag pattern through the churchyard. They ended their pattern along one wall of the church.

"I think we're good to go." Before Phil could continue his thought, he looked past his friends. "Oh no. Quick. Follow me," he said.

Del glanced in the direction Phil had been looking. There, walking toward the church was the priest with another man and two women. Phil raced along the side of the building to a concrete staircase that led down to a small door. The others followed and they all descended. Phil tried the handle. Nothing.

"I think we should be okay," said Phil. "I don't think they saw us." He snuck up the stairs and peaked out. "Shoot. They're coming this way."

"Should we make a run for it?" asked Guy.

"No," said Phil. "I've got a better idea." He pulled out a small pry bar and hammer from the bag he was carrying.

"You're not going to break into a church?" Del said, not liking where this was heading.

Phil looked at her intently. "Did you see a magic glass in the ground or not? If we're going to dig it up today, we better make sure that the priest doesn't see us."

"I didn't say it was a magic glass. I just said it glowed," Del said. "And who said anything about digging it up? I just want you guys to see it."

"Sure sounded magic to me," Phil said. "Who knows what it might be. We are going to have to get a good look at it." And with that, Phil had the pry bar in place. He gave it three quick whacks with the hammer, and the door miraculously popped open. Had he done this sort of thing before? Not to any of his friends' knowledge.

Phil walked into the dark basement, then turned to look back over his shoulder. "C'mon," he said. He went inside, followed by Guy.

"You sure about this?" Sam said to Del.

Del nodded, and the two remaining friends entered the building.

*****

They closed the door behind them putting themselves in thick darkness. Each of them whipped out their phones and used them as flashlights to find their way. Guy found a light switch and turned it on. The basement was much nicer than any of them imagined.

The walls were bright orange and green. There were colorful posters on the wall. The room was clearly for kids. There was a brightly tiled floor in one section and carpet in another. Books and craft supplies lined one of the walls. Del was surprised. The room looked... fun. What was a room like this doing in a dusty old church? It was weird.

"Turn the lights off!" Phil ordered. "If they see the lights on we'll be in trouble. C'mon; let's head upstairs."

They found the staircase and headed up. The main floor had some natural light filtered through some old yellow tinted windows. They didn't need their phone lights anymore. This floor was much less fun looking than the basement. Nothing was new about the place. There were old pictures of all the priests that had worked there over the years. There were wall hangings that looked ancient. There was a massive picture of a guy with long brown hair, blue eyes, with milky white skin and wearing a flowing white shirt.

"I think this guy must have been important in the 1960s or 70s," said Guy, "He looks like some of my grandma's pictures. She called them hippies."

"That's Jesus," Sam said. Sam went to church most weeks with his family, but he'd never admit it to the guys. He went to a more modern one on the other side of town. Del knew, but also knew enough to not tell Phil or Guy.

"How do you know it's Jesus?" Guy asked.

"It looks like Jesus. That's just what he looks like," said Sam.

"Seems freaky to me," concluded Guy.

"Shut up," said Phil. He led them to the large wooden doors on the far side of the building and unlatched the three brass locks. "You said that the hedge was a good hiding place?" he asked Del.

Del nodded.

"If the priest and the others are still on the other side of the church, we should be able to run from here to the hedge without being seen. Once we're under it, we should be good, right?"

"I'm pretty sure we'll be well hidden under the hedge," said Del.

"Okay," Phil continued. "When I open the door, Del will take the lead. You know where to go. Get us under that hedge without being seen."

Del nodded again.

*****

Phil swung open the door. Del took a quick look around. There was no sign of anyone. She took off as quickly as she could toward the hedge. As she reached it, she swung around to run exactly the way she had the day before. The small hole in the hedge presented itself, and she dove through it. She rolled out of the way, knowing the others were right behind her. Guy, Sam, followed by Phil, all flew into the small clearing under the massive hedge.

"We're good," said Phil. "No sign of anyone. So, where is it?"

"I don't know; it was right here yesterday," said Del, looking around at the ground frantically.

"Like I said yesterday," said Phil. "I knew this was going to be lame. The glass thing isn't even here."

Del lay on the gravestone face down and stared at the name "BLYTHE".

"What are you doing?" said Guy. "That's somebody's... well... there's a dead guy under there."

"Maybe if I do exactly what I did yesterday, the glass will appear," said Del.

"You're crazy," said Phil, his impatience clearly growing. "Things don't just appear in the ground. C'mon Deli; there's nothing here. Get up."

Del hated when her sister or Jerk called her that, but it was even worse when it was her friends.

"Shut up, Philly Cheesesteak!" Del looked up as she shouted and saw the glass embedded in the ground just as it had been yesterday.

"Hold on. Here it is!" she declared.

All three of the boys looked on in disbelief.

"What did you do?" said Phil. "Things don't just appear out of nowhere."

Del moved a shaking hand toward the glass and touched it. The glow happened just as before.

"Magic things do," she said.

"Holy! What is that?" said Guy.

The boys stood motionless and speechless for a minute. Then Phil emptied the contents of his bag. There were small hand shovels, trowels, the pry bar, a hammer, and a knife.

"Let's get to work," Phil said as he grabbed a trowel and started digging around the glass.

"Are you sure we should do this?" Sam asked. "If it is magic, maybe it should be left alone. Besides, it's not ours."

Guy and Del ignored him and picked up tools to help Phil.

Phil worked fast, but the glass was larger than they had thought. Eventually they found an edge and began digging deeper.

"I think maybe I can pry it up," said Phil.

He slipped his hand underneath one edge of the glass and gave it a tug. In response, the light flashed and glowed as before, but slightly free from the grip of soil and grass, the glass shuddered. Phil recoiled, pulling his hand away.

The glowing light within the glass did not die down and neither did its shaking. The light got brighter and moved around within the glass much more than before. The shaking got more intense, until the light broke free from the glass. A focussed beam of light shot up and out of the glass and fanned out to make an oval shape in the air, perpendicular to the ground. The bottom of the oval hovered a few inches off the ground, and the top was just a hair lower than Guy's head. The light of the oval was all different colors. None of them had ever seen anything like this. The magic of the glass had been unleashed.

"What do we do now?" said Guy.

"I don't know," said Del. "This didn't happen yesterday."

"No kidding," said Guy. "I think Del should touch it and see what happens."

"Why me?" said Del.

"It's your glass; you found it," said Phil.

"You're the one who got it mad and made it do this whole oval energy shield thing," said Del.

Just then Sam threw a small rock at the oval of light, and the rock disappeared.

"Probably a good thing you didn't touch it, Del" said Phil with a laugh.

Sam walked up to the oval.

"Sam, no! What are you doing?" Del said, thinking that of all of them Sam was most likely to walk right into it; he often seemed as though he wanted to disappear.

He held up a small twig and touched it to the oval. The twig was ripped out of his hand and pulled into the light. Gone.

"What is this thing?" said Phil.

Sam seemed intrigued and was looking for more stuff to disintegrate. Del was worried.

Suddenly, Del became aware that there were more than the four of them under the hedge.

"I see you've found our little secret."

It was the priest.

CHAPTER THREE
The Priest's Riddle

Phil, Guy, Del, and Sam, with no clue what to do, remained frozen in place. Surrounded by bush with the only entrance to the clearing blocked by the priest, they could not attempt a getaway. Their paralysis may have also been due to the priest's claim that the floating oval of light was his "little secret." The priest knew about this hiding place, knew about the glass, and knew about the light that could come out of it. Of all the people in the clearing, the priest seemed the least surprised by what was going on, and this just added to the shock of the four children.

"It's okay," the priest began. "There's nothing to fear. You have found something wonderful and beautiful here under the thicket."

The kids always ran whenever they saw the priest. The boys had never taken a moment to look back, but Del always did. He always wore the same smile. She had always seen it from a distance in a fleeting sort of way and had assumed it was a creepy kind of smile. But now, up close, all she could sense was warmth and kindness. In an instant, all of the encounters with the priest came flying back to her. He only ever managed to get about one word out before the children ran. Usually it was some variation on "hello." He had never yelled after them. He had never looked angry. Perhaps they had been wrong about him all the times they had run in and out of his churchyard. Del thought of the basement of the church with its bright colors and fun atmosphere. If he had that kind of place in his church, maybe he wasn't so bad.

Phil found some courage and spoke up. "You said *our* little secret. Who else knows about this?"

"I do, dear," said a voice. And from behind the priest, up through the entryway came one of the women whom they had seen walking with the priest in the churchyard. She had the same kind look as the priest and looked about his age. In all the years they had been running from the priest, they had never seen this woman until this morning.

"How rude of me," the priest said. "Let me introduce you to my wife. Come to think of it, I'm not sure I've ever introduced myself, and now we are going to have to know one another, especially with your discovery. This will most certainly change everything for you, and you will need our help if you are going to go in." He nodded in the direction of the oval of light.

"I'll do the introductions," said the woman. "We're Mr. and Mrs. Manters."

"You're allowed to get married?" Guy blurted out.

"Yes, of course," Mrs. Manters replied. "We're not Catholic. We're Lutheran." This meant nothing to the children who stared at them blankly.

"Catholic priests are forbidden from getting married,

but Mr. Manters is a Lutheran pastor. Lutherans, Presbyterians, Anglicans, Pentecostals, Baptists - all their clergy can get married. We've been happily married for 43 years."

Sam nodded as Mrs. Manters spoke, taking it in. He, of course, knew what she was talking about. He went to a Baptist Church. It wasn't clear why he thought the man who always chased them was a Catholic priest. Perhaps it was just Mr. Manters' age, and the fact that Phil and Guy had started calling him "the priest."

"Surely you don't want to ask us about being married," the priest jumped in. "I'm guessing you want to know about the light."

The children nodded.

"The light behind you is a door through which you must pass. And when you pass through that door, your lives will be forever changed."

*****

"When Sam throws stuff at it, it totally disappears!" said Phil. "I'm not touching that thing!"

"Naturally, the items disappear," said the priest. "They will have passed through to the other side, and I strongly encourage each of you to step through as well. You will not regret it. I simply insist that now that you've found the light, you must go through."

Sam moved a little bit towards it.

"Don't even think about it, Sam!" said Phil.

Del cut him off. "But we're all thinking about it, aren't we? We're all wondering a little." She turned toward the priest and his wife. "What exactly is on the other side?"

"That I cannot tell you. You must experience it for yourself. But know that once you take the step through the light, you will never be the same. You will find your way back into this world, but you will be a different person when you return."

"That's crazy!" said Phil. "Even if it's true that it's a door and not something that will just kill us on the spot, I'm not going through to be changed. I don't want to be any different than I already am."

The priest just smiled. "Of course you don't, but I'm not sure your friends can say the same. And, crossing into this world is not about the change you desire or don't desire - it is about the change that you need. Each of you will change for better or for worse as you grow older. Now is the time when you can choose the right kind of change. Now is the time when you must take the steps that will affect your lives for the good."

The children wore looks of confusion and suspicion. The priest continued. "I have been keeping an eye on you for many years. The four of you care about one another. You are good ages to make the journey for the first time. You will work together and stand by each other through thick and thin. I had just made up my mind to talk with you, to encourage you to take the journey, when yesterday, by such wonderful providence, you, Delaney, slid under the thicket and found this place."

Del was taken aback that the priest knew her full name.

He continued on, "You four - Phillip Coons, Guillome Thompkins, Samuel Long, and Delaney Ryder - are such good friends. You will need each other, not just on the other side, but when you return. This is part of why it is important that you all go together. We need young ones like yourselves to carry on for us after we are gone. Our time is running out. I can see you have doubts and that is very normal, but this is the time to overcome doubt. This is where you must face the fear of the unknown. I can help you with the most significant fear. I'll go through myself, and show you that it is quite safe to travel from our world into the other one."

Mrs. Manters protested. "This would have to be your last time. You can't go again." She turned to the children "You see, while it is safe, when you are older, the journey takes a lot out of you. You're fine as children, but we've been through so many times that we are reaching our limit." She looked back at her husband. "Don't go just to prove to them that you can return. Save your last time for when we can go together."

Then she leaned closer and whispered in her husband's ear, something barely audible but that Del heard. "What if you can't get back?"

"I will return without any scratch or scathe," the priest announced.

He squeezed past the children, and before they knew it, he had reached out his hand and touched the oval of light. Upon being touched, the oval bent a little bit, and then to the children, it looked like it sucked the priest through.

They stood there in silence for a few seconds, and then the light turned off. The oval of light completely disappeared. They looked down at the piece of glass in the ground with no beams coming out of it. Del jumped down and touched the top of it. No light.

"How did you get the oval, I mean, the door to appear before, Phil?" Del asked.

Phil knelt down beside Del, shoving her out of the way slightly. He put his hand on the glass exactly as before and pulled. Nothing.

"What now?" Phil said.

"We wait," said Mrs. Manters.

*****

Del was starting to worry about the time. Her sister might have woken up by now and would be starting to get angry that Del had touched her phone. She most likely would have texted Jerk and they would be heading down to the churchyard to find her. Fortunately, they were in the single best hiding spot in the whole churchyard; it's just that Del knew that Jerk would tear the place apart. She had been beginning to think that stepping through the portal might be a convenient way to escape her sister, but now the door had disappeared. As Del looked over at the priest's wife, she was sure she wore a look of sadness and concern. She was probably doubting whether she would see her husband again.

"How long do we wait?" Del said.

"Not much longer now," said Mrs. Manters.

"This is ridiculous!" exclaimed Phil. "The priest just killed himself by touching the light. We can't get the light back, and we're just sitting here doing nothing. For what?"

"In the hope that the priest... I mean... In the hope that Mr. Manters will return." Del said. "Have some respect, Phil. It's her husband."

Phil sat down, and the wait continued. But Phil was

anything but patient. "That's it, I'm done. I'm going home," he said.

"No you're not." It was the priest's voice, and it came from the glass.

The phrase had barely been heard when the stone shook and glowed, the beams of light shone up, the oval of light appeared, and out he stepped. Mrs. Manters's face was almost as bright as the stone's light when she saw her husband. He raced over to her and gave her a hug and kiss as though they had been apart for months.

"I was really starting to worry," said Mrs. Manters. "You were gone so long this time."

"Gone so long?" said Del. "We were worried and everything, but it was only ten minutes."

The couple gave each other a knowing look, a look that the children would eventually understand.

The priest turned to the children. "There. I've returned, and I'm fine. It took a little longer than planned, but here I am. And the four of you can get ready to go yourselves. As you can see, you'll be back quite soon."

Guy looked at his friends "What do you think, guys? Should we do it? Phil?"

In a rare moment, Phil looked at Sam and Del and asked them their opinions. "What do you guys think?"

Del looked at Sam, and Sam spoke up. "I think for some reason we were brought here. I feel like we were meant to find this."

"I say we go through," said Del.

Phil stood up and made the announcement to the priest. "We'll go."

"Splendid!" said the priest.

*****

The priest gave them instructions. "You'll need to hold onto each other as you travel through the door. This is of the utmost importance. You don't want to lose each other." The priest looked far more serious now that the decision to go through had been made.

"Seriously, what are we going to see on the other side?" Guy asked.

"It is less about what you will see with these," said the priest, pointing to his eyes, "and more about what you will see with this." The priest pointed to his heart.

Mrs. Manters cut in. "What he means is that it will be better for you to discover things for yourself."

"Stop interrupting," said the priest. "What I say is what I intend to mean. In any case, they should only know what I say, not what you might think I mean. Now look, you've gotten me all befuddled!" The priest looked even more serious. "There is one last thing you must remember before you enter the portal."

The children's eyes widened as the priest leaned in close to them, hushing his voice to a whisper. "Come now; join hands." Phil bent down to collect his tools.

"You won't need those," the Priest said. "And you'll be back in no time - they will be right here under the thicket where you left them. Now join hands and listen. You must remember what I say word for word."

The priest leaned closer to the four children and recited a poem.

Carry yourselves beyond the number
Through the place of the tallest lumber.
Seek the one from whom under you slid
Whose name you found when only you hid.

Within this one's fence, the door shall appear.
You won't see if you look, but you will if you hear.

"What on earth?" said Phil. Before Phil could get any more words out, the priest was pushing them in pairs, holding hands, into the light. First Phil and Del, followed by Guy and Sam.

"Have a wonderful journey!" The priest shouted after them.

Strangely, as soon as Del touched the light, everything went dark. Del felt Phil's grip on her hand tighten. The darkness felt like nothing Del had felt before. It was as if she wasn't anywhere. It was a very odd and somewhat dreadful feeling, because one simply is not used to being nowhere. There was the sense that in being nowhere you could almost choose to go anywhere you wished. Del tried to wish for where she'd like to go, but wasn't quite sure where that would be. Before she could think any further, they fell out of the total darkness. They were definitely somewhere - but where?

CHAPTER FOUR

Separated

Del was immediately aware of trees surrounding her. They were different than the trees at home - shorter, leafier, but there was something else about them as well. The leaves and the trunks of the trees appeared to be glowing. It was very gentle and light - almost unnoticeable. She looked up and saw a deep black sky. It must be the middle of the night here, she thought, and it must be cloudy. There were no stars and no moon. It would have been completely dark but for the glow from the trees. Del took this all in before she realized that she was still holding hands with Phil.

It was Phil who first noticed what was most important. Dropping Del's hand, he asked, urgently, "Where are Sam and Guy?"

Before Del could say anything, Phil was on the hunt. "They can't be far," he said, looking around feverishly. Then he called out, "Guy! Sa…"

"Shhh," Del stopped him. "We have no idea what else might be out there. We can't be yelling like that."

Phil agreed with a nod of his head and lowered his

voice to a whisper. "Sam? You there? They've got to be here somewhere."

Being in the middle of a forest made it difficult to conduct a good search, but Del and Phil pressed on. There was absolutely no sign of Guy or Sam, but Phil and Del didn't panic. The immediacy and urgency of the task at hand only served to bring them focus. They had never worked so well together.

"Look at this," said Phil. He had grabbed a leaf that was large enough that it could have covered both Sam and Guy. The place that he held with his hand glowed more than the rest of the leaf.

"Look at this," Phil repeated. "It glows when you touch it."

"The whole place is glowing," said Del.

Phil looked around as though he was only just noticing the glow from within the plants and trees.

"But it glows more when you grab one," he said.

He brushed some of the larger leaves aside, and grabbed the trunk of a tree with both hands and squeezed hard. The tree glowed in proportion to the pressure applied. The tree did not emit brighter light, but it glowed more intensely, more deeply.

As the light swirled within the trunk, every leaf on it lit up. The tree was massive, with hundreds of leaves larger than either of the children, many of them larger than any grownup. Phil squeezed harder and harder until suddenly there was a kind of coughing sound. The sound rumbled deep. Then the branches above let out several creaks and, although there was no wind whatsoever, the leaves rustled loudly.

"I think you should let go of that tree," Del said to Phil.

The tree let out a low moan as a long branch whipped just past Del's head. Phil let go of the trunk.

"Run!" Del cried.

She and Phil took off into the forest. Phil streaked ahead, once again with no concern for Del. When he ran, he ran.

"We've got to stay together," Del called after him.

Phil slowed down a little.

"What was that thing?" Phil asked.

"I don't know. But I didn't want to stay around to find out."

As they ran, the landscape of the forest flew by. Trees and plants of various kinds, all glowing. The children made a terrible racket in their running through the forest, and things around them were starting to rouse. A bird with incredible red feathers flew out from under their feet, up and behind them. Then another bird, this time green. Then another - blue. Soon they were running surrounded by glowing leaves and branches under a canopy of red, green and blue glowing birds. And the birds were not quiet. They did not sing a sweet song; it was more like squawking.

The darkness in the sky was giving way to the first light of day while the birds swooped low. As Del and Phil ran their legs off through the forest, they could hear sounds coming from the trees. There was creaking, rustling, coughing, grunting, and sighing coming from every direction.

"They sound like my grandpa when he's waking up," said Phil.

The noise of the forest increased. Accompanying the sounds, the branches of the trees were moving in ways that only a living creature could move. The sight was terrifying as the trees appeared to be coming to life.

Phil and Del kept running, trying to keep in one direction, but found their path often blocked. Some branches came up to trip them; others swooped down from above to create barriers that they needed to duck under. The trees were succeeding in slowing them down. The children kept going, hoping that nothing would grab at them. Large leafy branches began swatting at them. Everything seemed to be moving in slow motion, the trees unable to keep pace with or anticipate Del and Phil's movements.

"We're faster than them," Phil said.

They dodged through the branches and leaves, but the forest only seemed to be getting thicker.

"We can't keep this up forever," Del said between heavy breaths.

"Just keep going," Phil said.

They started to slow a little. Then a little more, until they were only just a hair faster than the trees' movements. Phil and Del were out-maneuvering them, but they weren't getting very far.

Del, exhausted, tripped on a branch and hit the ground.

"Ouch!" she cried.

Phil stopped and saw a giant leaf falling down on top of her.

"Lookout!" he yelled as he leaped back to grab it. The leaf was way stronger than he was, but the distraction provided just enough of an opportunity for Del to roll to one side as the leaf just missed her. Del winced in pain as she twisted out of the way of the giant leaf. Phil grabbed her outstretched hand and pulled her to her feet. Together they got moving again.

"You okay?" Phil said.

"I think so," Del replied. "Something on the ground got me."

"What do mean?"

"Stung me, I think. But, I'm okay." Del didn't want to let on that the pain from whatever it was on the forest floor was very real. Something had stung her in the side, near her ribs. She hoped she was alright.

They went a little further and saw ahead what looked like a wall of leaves. "Do you think we can get over it?" asked Del.

"Or maybe through it," said Phil.

They each found one last burst of energy and raced toward the wall of leaves. As they got closer, they saw that it wasn't absolutely sealed. There were some small holes. If they were agile enough, they might be able to dive through. Del gave no thought to what might be awaiting them on the other side of the wall. She didn't care. Her only thought was - get out.

Phil, of course, got there first and dove head first toward one of the holes. Del saw him pass straight through. At the last second, Del saw a hole at the very bottom of the wall. She did a baseball slide, feet first, and burst through to the other side.

*****

The light of day beyond the leaf wall through which Phil and Del had emerged was dazzling. They lay, squinting and blinking, in what looked like very normal grass, trying to catch their breath. The grass belonged to a large open meadow that stretched out over rolling hills as far as their eyes could see.

Del ran her hand over her side where she had been stung. It was tender. Trying not to show Phil, she lifted her shirt to take a look, expecting to see a red bump similar to the one she had gotten when she was stung by a wasp the previous summer. There was some redness and a bit of swelling, but in a circle around the bump was a pale green ring with what looked like tiny green veins running out of it. It was sore, but bearable, so Del decided to keep it to herself. Phil wasn't the kind of guy that would ask about her sting. Not because he was uncaring, but because if someone said they were okay in the moment, then they were okay. Del had managed to conceal the entire inspection of her side as the whole time Phil had been staring intently at the plant wall through which they had just dived.

"Do you think Guy and Sam were in there?" asked Phil.

"Probably. I hope they made it out," said Del.

She pulled out her phone to check the time and to see if she could text Sam or Guy. "It's dead," she said.

"Mine too," said Phil, checking his as well. "Weird - I've barely used it today."

Del played around trying to reset her phone. Nothing happened. It was completely gone.

"Maybe they just don't work here," she concluded. "Wherever here is."

They put their phones away, and Phil gazed at the forest again.

"There's no way Sam got out of there," he said.

"Don't say that!" said Del. "Guy would have got them out. And if he did, Sam would insist that once they were safe, they shouldn't move. They should just wait for help. Sam would know we would come for him."

"I guess looking for them is the only thing we can do," said Phil. "Our best bet is going to be to walk around the edge of the forest, but which way?"

"There are only two choices," Del said. "Left or right."

After making their choice, Del and Phil started walking along the edge of the forest. They walked in silence for a long time. There was no sign of Sam or Guy, nor was there any wildlife, nor any change in the foliage; just the forest on their left and the rolling meadow on their right. Along the way, Phil kept glancing at the forest and looking over his shoulder.

"Do you feel like something is watching us?" asked Phil.

"I do now!" said Del.

As they continued on, the feeling of being watched grew inside her. She kept checking the forest and noticed Phil checking it as well. Several times, Del thought she had seen something, and each time she took an extra breath. She told herself that there were probably squirrels or birds in the forest and that they were probably more scared of Phil and her than she and Phil were of them. This is what she told herself, but she didn't quite believe it.

They kept walking, never breaking their unspoken rule of not talking about what might be following them.

"How big do you think this forest is?" asked Del.

"Dunno," said Phil.

They walked some more. Del's mouth was getting very dry and the pain in her side was getting worse.

"Do you think we should keep going?" asked Del.

"I don't know what to do any better than you do,"

said Phil.

They walked some more. They climbed several small hills, and each time, Del hoped that there would be something different on the other side. Even a curve of the forest or a thinning out of the trees would have been welcome, but everything stayed basically the same. After hours of monotony, they climbed a hill that looked like all the others, but this time, when they got to the top of it, they saw something different. At the base of the hill coming out of the forest and meandering through the meadow was a small stream.

Del and Phil ran down the hill as fast as they could and, on arriving at the water, knelt down and cupped their hands, ready to quench their thirst.

"Wait," Del said. "How do we know it's safe?"

"We don't," said Phil. "But what choice do we have?"

As she looked into the stream, Del saw a glow similar to the glow of the trees and to the glass that she had found in the graveyard. The glow was no longer intriguing to her after having been attacked by the trees. Rather, it made her worry about drinking it. But Phil was right - they had no other choice. They needed to drink. They both reached down, pulled up a handful of water and gulped it down.

It was fantastic: sweeter than water, like drinking a soft drink without the bubbles, but not that terrible flat taste you usually get when soft drinks have lost their fizz. With just the first mouthful, Del felt her energy being renewed and felt some of the pain in her side subside. Was this just what water tasted like when you were that thirsty? No. It was more than that. There was something else to it. They both went back for more.

"It's like drinking an energy drink," Phil said.

"Ya - but it tastes good," said Del.

"Better than good."

"Better than fantastic."

The two children sat, satisfied. Somehow, after drinking the water, any hunger Del had been experiencing had disappeared as well.

"Do you think we should follow the stream through the meadow?" Phil asked.

"I don't know," said Del. "Going around the forest isn't getting us anywhere, and I don't know how we are ever going to find Guy and Sam."

"If they found this stream maybe they followed it," Phil suggested.

"We are so far from where we started. I don't know if they would have found this," Del said. "I do know they would stay put, even for hours. Sam would insist."

Del knew, and she was sure Phil did too, that Guy acted tough, but if Sam resolved to do something, he would not let it go.

"So what do you think we should we do?" Phil asked.

"I think we should turn back," said Del. "I mean, what if they just got out of the forest and went the other direction. Maybe we should have gone right instead of left."

"That's gotta be at least three hours back!" said Phil.

"I know. But it's our only shot at finding them today."

Phil nodded in agreement.

Del continued: "If we can, we need to find a way to carry some water with us for the trip. I wish we had a bottle or something."

They started looking around for something they could use as a container. Since the meadow was unlikely to yield anything, they went as close to the edge of the forest as they dared to conduct their search. After their energy water, the forest seemed to become much more peaceful in Del's eyes. The whole place had its own glow beyond the light of day. The light from the river and trees seemed to interact with each other as though they were passing messages back and forth. Del and Phil were careful not to get close enough for a leaf to touch them. They searched intently, but nothing could be found to carry water in.

Del looked as deeply as she could into the forest, letting her eyes follow the path of the stream. Far away, on the bank, there was a red glow that seemed to move along the forest floor. Something was coming toward them.

"What is that?" Del whispered.

"I don't know," said Phil. "But I don't think we should wait around here to find out."

He turned to get away from the glow of the forest and into the full light of the meadow. As soon as Phil turned, the red glow disappeared.

"Phil, look," Del said.

Phil turned back to see two red eyes peering at them from just inside the forest.

*****

Phil and Del froze in place not wanting to make a move in case the eyes belonged to a predator. Locked in a staring contest, the owner of the unblinking red eyes emerged ever so slowly from the shadows. A strange looking creature stood before them. It stood a little over waist-high. Its head was disproportionately large compared to its body, with its large, red eyes spaced far apart. It wore simple tan colored fabric clothes. The children might have called it a gnome or an elf, but it didn't quite fit any of the descriptions of such fantasy creatures. Del took a very small step towards it.

"It's okay," she said.

The creature made a kind of chirping sound back at her and stepped toward her. It made motions in, what looked like, a peaceful sort of way. It held out an open hand to Del. Del moved closer, continually saying things like "We're not going to hurt you" and "Gentle, gentle." The whole time the creature made its chirping sounds. They got close enough to touch each other and each reached out their hands. Their fingertips touched. Del's eyes widened, and Phil gasped as a red glow welled up within the creature, visible even through the creature's clothes.

"No!" Phil yelled, fearing the worst for Del.

He jumped toward her and grabbed her other arm, pulling her away. It was as though Phil had broken a kind of trance. Phil and Del took off following the stream away from the forest. The creature waited for a minute, then jumped into the water. The red glow zoomed through the stream faster than anything, and without missing a beat, the creature jumped out of the water into the air, landing on its feet right in front of Phil and Del.

"It's okay. I'm not going to hurt you. Gentle, gentle." The creature spoke English.

As it spoke, it grabbed both Phil and Del by the arms and held them tightly.

"It's okay," the creature repeated.

"I don't think so," said Phil as he struggled to get free.

As Del worked at peeling away the creature's hand

from its grip on her, she could not believe what she saw. All the fingers on the hand were webbed, perfect for swimming quickly in water. She glanced at the feet, and they were webbed too. Then she watched as the feet turned into regular feet, the hands turned into regular hands, and the creature's hair and clothes magically became dry. Its transformation didn't stop there. It started getting larger, beginning with its hands, then the arms, the torso and legs, until it looked very much like a person.

If it wasn't for the red eyes and the strange red glow coming from within, and if they had just met this creature now, Del and Phil would have concluded that it was a boy of about twelve years of age. There was no more chirping. The only sounds it made were English. The repeated "I'm not going to hurt you" and "It's okay" were its refrain as the transformation continued.

"Stop struggling!" it said. "I'm going to let you go, but you have to promise not to run. I'm going to sit over here, and we can just talk. I'll tell you who I am, but I need to know who you are. This is important because I think you might have been sent here to help us."

It released its grip, and said again, very gently "Are you here to help us?"

As soon as the grip loosened, Phil took off, but Del stood her ground. "Phil! Come back!"

Phil stopped and turned back to Del. "No Del, c'mon. We've got to get away from this thing."

"We're going to be okay," Del replied. "He might be able to help us. I want to talk."

Del looked pleadingly at Phil, who walked back, defeated. He slumped down on the ground.

"Fine. Let's talk," he said.

CHAPTER FIVE

Back Into the Forest

Phil, Del and the red-eyed creature-turned-boy sat in the meadow next to the stream on the edge of the glowing forest. Del took it upon herself to begin in a polite sort of way.

"My name's Del, and this is Phil," she said.

"I'm Crimson," said the creature. "You are here to help us, right?"

"I think we probably need your help more than you need ours," said Del. "But first - how did you... do all that?"

"All what?"

"The... changing."

"That's just what we lumens do. We use the light to change our shape into anything we touch. I'm young so I'm still learning. I just broke through on languages this year. So, when I touched you I can turn into something that looks like you, but I can also speak your language."

"The chirping?" asked Del.

"That's the lumen language."

"What's a lumen?"

"I'm a lumen. There are lots of us, but we are losing light - everyone is. That's why we need your help. I'm sure you've been sent to us, because you're... well... most lumens think you are legends."

"What do you mean we're legends?"

"We call you the Malak. There are legends about how you came many years ago and helped rescue all of Azdia from the dark times. And now our light is fading, and you've come again!"

"Hold on, slow down - we've never been here before!"

"You haven't?" Crimson thought for a minute. "No, of course *you* haven't. But there are others like you."

"Of course there are, but..." Del stopped and for the first time since landing in the middle of the forest, she thought of the priest and his wife. "Yes - there are others who came here before us. Perhaps they helped you back then, but we don't know anything about that. And right now, it's us who need your help, and it's more urgent than your light, and we're wasting time."

Crimson looked a little taken aback.

"I'm sorry," Del said, realizing that the fading light was probably the most important thing in the world to this creature, and she had basically just said she didn't care.

"Look," Del tried again."We're just really worried because we got separated from our two friends and we don't know where they are. We need to find them."

Crimson seemed to brighten at this. "You mean there are more of you!"

Phil had been sitting on the grass looking a little stunned as this conversation had gone on. "What's Azdia?" he said suddenly.

"Oh. Pardon me," said Crimson. "I assumed you would know. This is Azdia." Crimson motioned all around them.

"The grass?" Phil said.

"No - this land. Everything. All the provinces. I really thought, as the Malak, you would know the place you are coming to save."

"This is all crazy talk!" said Phil.

Del had to jump back in before Phil damaged the tenuous relationship developing between Crimson and themselves. "It's okay. We'll get everything figured out. Crimson - maybe we just call Azdia by a different name - right, Phil? Just like you call us Malak."

"THE Malak," Crimson cut in.

"Yes, the Malak. But we call ourselves human. We've never heard the word Malak before."

"So what do you call Azdia?"

"We call it…" Del tried to think fast.

"Australia!" Phil jumped in with a laugh.

Del flashed an angry look at Phil.

"That sounds like a magical place!" said Crimson.

Phil smirked at Del. Del thought that if this Crimson believed they were the saviours of his world, then they could probably convince him to help find Sam and Guy. She continued trying to sound as though she had some authority.

"We'd like to help you if we can," Del said. "But it is important that we find our two friends. Will you help us?"

"Two more Malak?" Crimson said. "Absolutely. When was the last time you saw them?"

"In the churchyard, just before coming here." Phil said.

Crimson looked confused.

"Phil means that the four of us all left together to come to Azdia from our world, but when we arrived, we were separated."

"And is 'churchyard' what you call your world?"

"Ya - that's right," said Phil.

This seemed to satisfy Crimson, so Del let it go.

"So we really have nothing to go on," said Del. "Except that we arrived in the forest somewhere, so they probably did too."

"That will do nicely. Let's go find them." Crimson began walking toward the forest. He called over his shoulder "What are their names?"

"Sam and Guy," Del replied. "But, where are we going?"

"You said they are probably in the forest, right?" said Crimson.

"I'm not going back in there!" Phil said.

"There's nothing to be afraid of. I'll just ask the trees if they've seen them. They probably have."

Phil and Del had looks of absolute horror on their faces. Crimson did not pick up on this.

"Come on!" he insisted. "You're the ones who didn't want to waste time."

"Those trees tried to kill us!" Phil said.

"No. The trees wouldn't hurt a fly." Crimson paused. "Hold on. You didn't wake them up, did you? I did hear them grumbling about being woken up early."

"It wasn't our fault," Phil blurted out. "How were we to know the trees would come alive?"

"If you make enough racket, why wouldn't they wake up? A grumpy early morning tree is not a pretty sight. I suppose you might have felt attacked, but I can assure you they are safe, basically. They are a little particular about anything new or different, but you're with me now, so we should be fine."

"I don't think this is a good idea," said Phil.

"He says he'll help us find Sam and Guy," said Del. "I think we have to trust him. What else can we do?"

"I just don't like the idea of going back into that forest."

"Me neither, but this might be our only chance to find Sam and Guy."

Although still clearly uncomfortable, as was Del, this seemed to settle it for Phil.

*****

Del and Phil followed Crimson into the forest, past the first trees, and were relieved when very little happened. The trees simply swayed the way trees do, creaked a little bit, their leaves rustling in the gentle breeze. After no more than about ten steps, Del grabbed Crimson's arm, leaned into him, and whispered as they walked.

"You said you were going to ask the trees where Sam and Guy are. Why don't you just talk to one of these trees right here?"

"The trees on the edge have less reliable information," Crimson whispered back. "The farther into the forest we go, the better chance we have of finding a tree that will actually know where the other Malak are."

"But can't we…"

"No. Shh." Crimson cut her off. "It might be best if you kept the talking to a minimum. The trees get startled when they hear unfamiliar sounds."

He stood motionless, signalling for Phil and Del to do the same.

"See how they are stirring?" Crimson whispered. "They will start to get agitated with too much noise. Now stay quiet, and follow me."

Del couldn't see any noticeable difference in the tree's demeanour - if trees could have a demeanour. Either Crimson could see something they couldn't, or he just wanted to keep them quiet for some other reason. Regardless, the children were now committed to this course of action. There was no turning back.

Without any chatter, or running, or disruption, it became much easier to notice what they likely missed in their earlier run out of the forest. There was so much to take in and no opportunity to ask their guide about what they saw.

Del began to see patterns in the stream next to them. Following the current of the stream were tiny little bugs that looked like miniature fireflies glowing different colors. It was easy to see how they might have been imperceptible in the full light of day, but in the gloom of the forest, their glow was clear. Had they drunk them? Had the bugs been what had tasted so sweet? She wasn't sure if the thought of drinking glow-bugs made her feel strong or gave her the creeps.

Then there were the variety of trees, each of them with a unique kind of glow to their trunks and leaves. Light was everywhere in this place. Everything that had a color glowed: leaves, moss, flowers. Everything looked exotic, unlike anything Del had ever seen, yet there was a sense of familiarity about it. It was, after all, still a forest.

Because of their stealth, they began to run across unique wildlife. Some would look up at them, curious. Others would run away, frightened. Most were just going about their routines, uninterested in any intrusion from outsiders. Every time Del saw an animal, she would compare it to something that she knew. It was her only way of making sense of what she saw: a large squirrel with a monkey's tail, a bird that hovered like a humming bird but had to have been the size of a bald eagle, a whole troop of cats with horns like that of a goat. None of the comparisons quite fit with what she saw, but they helped her make some sense of this extra-sensory world in which she found herself.

After walking for some time in silence, Crimson signalled for them to stop. He pointed up ahead to an area where the forest thinned out. There were five massive creatures. Del immediately thought of a cross between an elephant and giraffe, just hairier.

The creatures stood on four thick legs and from their hoofs to the top of their backs must have been about six feet. Their bodies were massive and grey; this was the part that looked most elephant-like. Each one had a long neck, indeed reminiscent of a giraffe's in length, but wider and stronger. Each neck extended out of sight, beyond the treetops, so that their heads remained hidden. Del didn't want to imagine what kind of heads might be perched on top their bodies.

"Let's ask them if they've seen anything," Crimson whispered.

"Are you serious?" Phil and Del protested together.

"Yes. You two stay here. Wouldn't want them to be afraid when they see you."

"Yeah - we wouldn't want the giant dinosaurs to be

afraid," said Phil.

Del thought Phil was right. They did look like big, hairy dinosaurs.

Crimson ignored them and simply walked over the animals and made a few chirping sounds. One giant head came swooping down. It was a sight to see. The face looked a little like that of a bird, or for that matter, a dinosaur. It had eyes on either side of its head, and a kind of beak for a mouth. It had obvious ears above its eyes and three massive antlers on top of its head, two on either side and one in the middle. When Del and Phil saw it, they both took a step back and gasped. At their gasp, it seemed like the wind blew a little stronger. The leaves rustled a little more, and the branches of the trees creaked.

The giant creature grunted and groaned as its head bent right down to tiny little Crimson. Crimson patted the side of the beast's face and then started making the same grunting, groaning noises. They grunted back and forth for several minutes until Crimson grabbed it by one of the antlers and swung himself up to sit just behind the central horn on its head. The neck bent back up and lifted Crimson up beyond the treetops.

Del and Phil looked at each other in disbelief.

"Should we do something?" Phil asked.

"What would we do?" said Del.

"I don't know. We could just follow the stream back out of the forest. I don't want to be in here at night."

"I know what you mean, but what if we're getting close to finding Sam and Guy."

"How can we even know if we're close? This creature, Crimson, has told us nothing, and now he's up there, with those things!"

Phil had a good point, Del thought. Maybe they should just turn back. But wouldn't turning back be giving up on their friends?

"I think we have to wait, Phil. I think we have to wait for Crimson."

"He could be leading us into some kind of trap."

"He could be, but he did talk to us. And I don't think he would make up the story about the Malak. I don't know why he would tell us all that if he didn't really believe it. If he didn't really believe that we could help him."

"But we can't help him, can we? We need him to help us. And what happens when he finds out that we aren't who he thinks we are? What happens if we find Sam and Guy, and then we can't do a thing to help him with his fading light?"

"I don't know. But if this is our only chance to find Sam and Guy, then we've got to take it."

They sat silently for a while, until Phil spoke again. "We don't even know how we're going to get back home. I thought we'd see a light-door or whatever it was on this side. I thought we'd just explore and jump back through whenever we wanted like the priest did."

As their conversation had progressed, they hadn't notice that the legs of one of the creatures had crept a little closer to them. Suddenly the head of the beast with Crimson on top was right next to them. Del screamed. So did Phil.

Quick as a whip, Crimson let out a massive bellow as he jumped off the head. The creature's roar was even louder than Crimson's and soon, the forest was filled with the sounds of high pitched screams and low, deafening bellows. The rest of the creatures' heads appeared in an instant.

Crimson shouted "Get on!"

Phil and Del, bewildered, did nothing.

Crimson shouted again, "Get on a feldroe! Now! The trees are descending. Get on one of the feldroes!"

The branches of the trees swept down at the children with a terrible creaking and rustling. The forest around them suddenly got dark and terrible and louder than a jet engine at take-off. Phil reacted quickly. He grabbed an antler and swung himself up on top the way he'd seen Crimson do it.

Crimson just kept yelling, "Get on a feldroe!"

Phil shouted to Del, "He's talking about the dinosaurs. Get on!"

Del was frozen in place. A huge leaf swung past her, missing her head by inches. The one that followed was a direct hit. She lay, out cold, on the ground.

"No!!!" Phil cried.

He jumped off his feldroe to try and pick her up. Crimson was not far behind him. The two of them, avoiding the flying leaves and branches, hoisted Del up onto Crimson's mighty beast.

"I've got her," Crimson said as he positioned her between the antlers atop the animal's head. "Go!"

Phil dove out of the way of a passing branch and swung himself up onto another feldroe's head. It ascended beyond the swinging trees. A few seconds later, the other feldroe heads appeared, including the one with Crimson and Del's limp body.

If the trees were swatting at the bodies of the feldroes, they certainly couldn't feel it riding high above the top of the forest.

"Is she okay?" Phil asked.

"She'll be alright. The tree just put her to sleep," said Crimson.

"Just put her to sleep? The thing almost knocked her head off."

"Oh no. Not at all. It's not the knock; it's the touch from the leaf that matters when the trees are worried. If they make enough contact, they will put the threat to sleep instantly. It wears off after a while. She'll be groggy, but fine. Trees never intend harm to anyone."

"It sure felt like harm with all that noise. What exactly happened back there?" Phil was indignant.

"You two screamed. The trees panicked."

"Well, you snuck up on us!" Phil looked around quickly, finally realizing where he was: on top of a massive head, holding an antler of a dinosaur-sized animal. "I can't take it up here. We've got to get down."

"I'm afraid the forest wouldn't be quite ready for you yet. You caused quite a ruckus down there. News of that will travel fast, I would think."

"What are you talking about? We caused a ruckus? It was you that just popped out of nowhere with this thing and scared us to death!"

"I'm sorry if we startled you. We didn't mean to. I had convinced our friends here to take you up for a look. In any case, no one's hurt. And we're all up here now. Del will wake up soon."

Crimson had a bit of a smile on his face as though this was all a little funny to him.

"Oh, I almost forgot," he continued. "Give your feldroe a pat every now and again to let him know you're friends."

Phil shook his head in disbelief and anger, but in the end, he found himself doing just what Crimson had asked. He patted the beast on the side of his head. The feldroe made a kind of purring sound, and even with Phil's total dislike for the situation, somehow the sound comforted him. Phil looked around, and the tops of the trees around them looked peaceful. As far as the eye could see, there were green tree tops and a beautiful blue sky.

The feldroes moved at a loping pace, but it was certainly quicker than what they had been doing with their short legs on the forest floor. They rode for a while; then Del started to stir.

"What a dream that was," she said as she rubbed her eyes. When she opened them fully, she remembered it was all real.

CHAPTER SIX

The Old Oak

Del continued to ride with Crimson.

"How long was I out?" Del asked.

"Not long," Crimson replied.

"How did we get up here? On these things?"

"They're called feldroes," said Phil. "And they are wicked cool. I'm calling mine Greymane."

"It's not a horse," Del said.

"I know - but cool name, right?"

Del wondered what had happened to Phil. He seemed relaxed and happy. It was so unlike him. She stared at him for a while. He patted Greymane, and she heard a purring sound.

Phil smiled and said "Attaboy. You're gonna get us out of this mess. That's right."

"You should really get on your own feldroe," Crimson said.

"No, I think I'd rather stay with you if that's okay."

Maybe it was being above the trees or just being out of that forest, but since waking up, she felt safe with Crimson, and it seemed to her that Phil felt safe atop

Greymane. Crimson gave her a smile, letting her know it was fine to stay put.

"Where are we heading? Have you talked to any trees yet?" Del was full of questions.

"No, but it's better than I'd hoped," Crimson replied. "We wouldn't have been able to make it very far on foot, but with the feldroes' help, we will be able to reach the wisest tree in the forest. If you look ahead, you can just about see it."

Del squinted into the distance. "Where?" she asked.

"Do you see that bump of green way off on the horizon that's a little taller than all the other trees?" said Crimson. "That's the Old Oak."

"Oak? You have oak trees?"

"Just the one. But I'm not surprised you recognize its name - it was planted by a Malak, like you, or so the story goes."

"What story?"

Del wanted to find out more about the Malak. After her conversation with Phil had been interrupted by the violence of the forest, she was worrying more about what would happen when they needed to tell Crimson that they couldn't help him or his people. She figured the more they could learn about whatever Crimson believed they were supposed to do, the better chance they would have of letting him down easy or maybe escaping if it came to that.

"This tale has been passed down for generations among the lumens," Crimson began. "Before the dark times, Azdia was a realm of beauty and light. All was cared for, and everything worked together."

"Paradise." Del said.

Phil rolled his eyes - he wasn't totally changed by his

new love for Greymane.

"Yes - paradise. It was perfect until a dark figure emerged unlike anything we had known before. His name was Mordlum. Where he came from no one knew. He was always cloaked - no one ever saw his face, but the appearance of his form struck fear into the heart of any lumen who beheld him. When the first lumens tried to touch him to talk to him and understand who he was, he turned them into creatures of darkness. They understood his language, but their lights went out, and they began speaking for him. At first there were just three, then nine, and eventually thousands of lumens who were changed to the darkness. Mordlum created great black clouds that blotted out the sun during the day. The glow that you now see at night - it was far more glorious before that first darkness came.

"Mordlum declared himself ruler of Azdia. Our ancestors didn't really know what that meant. We had never had a ruler before. Mordlum was the first, and he was very pleased with that fact. He proclaimed that he had brought order to a world of chaos, but this just meant darkness to the lumens. He developed a way to remove light from all living things, and then he dispatched his converted lumens to begin the removal. He outlawed shape changing and language learning. Any lumen caught doing these things was banished to a place that Mordlum called the outer darkness. He would tell his victims that the darkness that had come to Azdia under his rule was nothing compared to the outer darkness that awaited anyone who disobeyed him.

"A group of dissenters to Mordlum's rule broke out, and they met in this very forest. And it was into the midst of that resistance that the first Malak was sent.

Her name was Eleanor. She gave them hope, telling them that, although it would take time, Mordlum would be defeated. He would be banished to the outer darkness, and the prisoners would be released."

Del, listening intently, said, "You said Eleanor was sent. Who sent her?"

"Ah, now that's the heart of the legend isn't it?" Crimson continued. "She was sent by the keeper of Azdia. In fact, before Eleanor's coming, the lumens had no name for the keeper although they knew there had always been one who kept and protected the light and beauty of our land. Eleanor taught us his name, but she did far more. She had been given an acorn by the keeper and had been told to plant it in the middle of this very forest. The keeper had told her that light would be restored to Azdia when the tree that grew out of that acorn outgrew the other trees of the forest. The keeper sent Eleanor as a messenger of light and a bearer of hope. I imagine that the keeper sent you?"

"I don't think so." Del thought that perhaps the priest was the keeper, and that perhaps Eleanor had come into Azdia the very same way they had come.

"Oh, you would know if Mr. Thicket had sent you," said Crimson.

"That's a weird name," said Phil.

"Why don't you go back to not listening!" said Del. "We don't know anyone by the name of Mr. Thicket. So that's the keeper's name?" She decided to keep the information about the priest to herself for the time being.

Phil slumped back down into Graymane as Crimson continued his tale. "Yes, yes. Mr. Thicket is his name. He is the keeper, the protector, the provider of Azdia.

He sent the Malak as our source of true light, the ones to fight against the darkness.

"Now Eleanor would only stay in Azdia for a few days or weeks at a time, to inspire the lumens and help them in their plans to restore the light and cast out Mordlum. Each year, the oak tree would get a little bit bigger, but Eleanor's visits got less and less frequent, sometimes going many, many years between visits. Many lumens gave up hope.

"After many years of absence, Eleanor returned to the Oak Tree and announced something that shocked everyone. She told them that she believed that the way to finally defeat Mordlum was not to cast him out, but to turn him away from the darkness and toward the light. At this, almost all of the most faithful lumens turned away from Eleanor and went to war against Mordlum's forces. Only fourteen remained true to Eleanor's vision, and it was these fourteen who became known as the Company of Light.

"Eleanor disappeared again for many years, and the lumens were divided. Light lost out to dark in terrible battles that the Company of Light believed never should have happened. The Oak Tree outgrew the other trees of the forest, and still Eleanor did not return. The lumen resistance had been decimated, but the Company of Light still remained hopeful. Finally, long after the Oak Tree had been planted, Eleanor returned, but this time she had someone with her - it was Mordlum. At the Oak Tree, Mordlum begged for forgiveness from the lumens, and the Company of Light granted it. Most other lumens did not forgive that easily, however. But there is great power in forgiveness, even if it is not everywhere, even if it is granted but by a small company. It was the forgiveness of the Company of Light that began pushing the darkness out. Eleanor, Mordlum, and the Company of Light travelled throughout Azdia telling everyone that the reign of darkness was over. They declared that Mordlum had renounced his throne and that light was returning. Eleanor and Mordlum stayed with the lumens for a long time bringing the light back. At the end of their time in Azdia, Mordlum announced his engagement to Eleanor, and, not long after, before leaving Azdia together, they were married under the Oak Tree, and the light was as fully restored as it is now."

"How long ago did this all happen?" Del asked.

Crimson thought for a moment. "It is an ancient tale. Think about how long it takes for an oak tree to grow and be old. The Old Oak has been old as long as I can remember. So how long ago did the Old Oak start being old? It's hard to say."

"So these trees are old? Like thousands of years?"

"Most of the trees are younger than the forest as a whole. You see, there are always new trees growing up, and older trees dying off. The Old Oak is by far the oldest tree still living. It has borne witness to almost everything that is known about Azdia and is, therefore, a tree of great wisdom. If any tree knows where your friends are, it is the Old Oak."

*****

As they got closer to the Old Oak, they could see that its height was significant. What looked like a small green blip from far away was in fact an expansive tree. It looked as though there were several oak trees growing out of the top of the forest, but these were simply its branches, which soared another twenty or twenty five feet above the canopy.

The feldroes stopped under the shade of a large leafy branch. Crimson grunted a few times to his feldroe, and it maneuvered in such a way that Crimson could grab on to one of the smaller branches. After latching on, Crimson and the Old Oak began to talk.

Their conversation was like nothing Del had ever seen before. The leaves of the tree would rustle, and the branches would creak. Then the same creaking and rustling sounds would come out of Crimson's mouth. They went back and forth for several minutes. Crimson let go and touched Del's arm.

"The Old Oak wants us to go down to the ground to get a better look at us," Crimson said.

"Was that all he said?" said Phil.

"It takes trees a long time to say anything," said Crimson.

The feldroes lowered their heads and let them off at the base of the Old Oak. Crimson grunted and groaned a few times and the feldroe grunted back.

"They need to be going." Crimson said.

"What are we going to do without them?" said Phil.

"We'll be fine," said Crimson. "Besides, they went above and beyond what we asked of them."

Phil took a moment to pat his feldroe. "Goodbye Graymane. I hope we will meet again."

The feldroes loped back in the direction from which they had come and were out of sight in no time. Phil looked down, shuffling his feet.

"You're not crying, are you?" said Del.

"No!" Phil turned away from her, rubbed his eyes

quickly and walked a few steps away.

"It might be best to let him be," said Crimson. "He had much longer with that feldroe than most creatures have in a lifetime. A powerful bond can be formed very quickly with feldroes, but I figured as a Malak he could handle it. He'll be okay."

Crimson turned back toward the Old Oak. "This might take a while," he said. "Trees talk slowly. Don't wander off, and definitely don't yell or anything. If you need me, signal to me. Just stay where I can see you."

Crimson walked over, and placed his hand on the trunk. The tree and lumen began creaking and rustling back and forth.

Phil had sat down on a nearby rock and stayed quiet.

Del looked around and thought about the legend Crimson had told. Was it true? Did all of it happen right here under this tree? The forest was more sparse here than in other parts of the forest. It felt much more like a clearing or a glade, despite there still being a completely covered canopy overhead. She found a large boulder with cut-out steps leading to the top of it. Maybe Eleanor made her speeches from the top of this rock. Del climbed the steps of the boulder and, from the top, she pictured hundreds of lumens like Crimson packed into the glade and a mighty warrior woman serving up hope with her words.

She wanted Crimson's story to be true. She wanted to be like Eleanor: bold, not afraid to do the difficult thing, respected, honoured, and most of all, loved. As Del stood on the rock, part of her wondered if she could be a Malak like Eleanor. Part of her wondered if she could help the lumens find their light again. She shook her head. They needed to find Sam and Guy and then find a way back home - that was all. At this thought, she went over to Phil.

"Phil, how are we going to get home?"

"I don't know," said Phil. "Maybe Sam will have an idea. He can usually figure things out. He likes mysteries and riddles and stuff."

"That's it!" exclaimed Del. "Remember what the priest told us to remember when we came through. It was a riddle. You're brilliant!"

"Thanks?" Phil looked confused. "The priest said something? I don't know if I was listening."

"Clearly not! But you're brilliant anyway! If I could just remember what he said." Del thought for a moment. "Go to the place with something number, something, something, tallest lumber. Sam will remember it for sure. He may even have it worked out! Do you think the riddle is our key to getting home?"

"Maybe we should ask Crimson to ask the Old Tree?" said Phil.

"No. We can't tell Crimson about this. Right now, he's helping us because he believes that we will help him. Once he knows we are just trying to go home, he won't want to help. And we need his help right now." Del outlined a plan for Phil. "Crimson helps us find Sam and Guy. Sam hopefully remembers the riddle. Solving the riddle gets us home."

"Hopefully?" said Phil.

"It's our best shot," said Del.

She had been keeping her eye on Crimson throughout their conversation. He stopped talking to the Old Oak, walked over to the children, and laid a hand on Phil's shoulder.

"I know where they are," Crimson said.

CHAPTER SEVEN

Finding Sam and Guy

Crimson was wearing a concerned look. "The Old Oak believes your friends are alright, but that they are being held captive."

"By who?" Phil said.

"By a group of trees."

"I don't get it," said Phil. "You keep telling us the trees are just easily startled or whatever. But now they've captured our friends! And the attacks on us have been way more than the trees just being worried about outsiders or being woken up."

"You're right," Crimson replied. He looked away, squinting into the depths of the forest as though searching for something. "When I saw the way the trees attacked you, I suspected something worse was going on but didn't want to say anything. The Old Oak feels the same way, however. The growing darkness is taking hold in the forest, and it is affecting the trees. While they've always been skittish about new things or situations, they are now talking as though anything unfamiliar is a threat. That's the exact word that the Old Oak used -

threat. The trees have only ever used that word once before - when Mordlum was ruling before he turned from dark to light."

"They think we're like Mordlum?" Del asked, wondering what this might mean for Sam and Guy who had been captured.

"No. What I mean is, that the trees only ever used the word 'threat' when they were under the influence of Mordlum. During his rule, there was the dark part of the forest, and there was the part of the forest under the protection of the Old Oak. The forest usually acts in total accord within itself, as any forest would do. But under Mordlum, the forest was at odds with itself. The Old Oak believes that the dark time is returning, and that a section of the forest is in the first stages of its light going out. It will begin with the trees rejecting anyone or anything unfamiliar or different and will eventually extend to us, the lumens."

"So, how do we save Sam and Guy?" Del asked.

"Your friends are not being held by dark trees, just scared, confused trees," Crimson continued. "The Old Oak thinks that the trees are keeping them until they can figure out whether they are a threat or not. The trees don't want to harm anyone, but they are very worried about the safety of the forest."

"How long will it take the trees to decide if Sam and Guy are a threat?" asked Del.

"And what will they do if they decide they are?" asked Phil.

"The trees won't act until they are sure, and that may take a very long time," Crimson replied.

"Do you have a plan?" asked Phil.

Crimson, still squinting through the trees, said, "The

plan is to get you something to eat and stay here for the night. It's getting late, and it will take most of the day tomorrow to get to the place where your friends are being held."

This made Del very anxious for their safety, but she was more anxious for poor Guy and Sam. They had been captured in the middle of the night by monster trees, and by the time Del and Phil got to them, they would have spent almost two days in captivity. Even once they found them, there was no guarantee of a successful rescue.

Crimson instructed Del and Phil to stay close to the Old Oak while he looked for some food. When he returned, he had an assortment of fantastic looking fruit, berries, and what looked like lettuce leaves.

"It's not much," Crimson said. "But it will do for tonight."

The ambient light of the forest was fading, and the glow within the leaves and branches was growing. They finished up their supper. Then Crimson encouraged them to rest.

"It will be best to sleep in the Old Oak," he said. "There are some good sleeping branches, and it's a pretty easy tree to climb."

"Does the Old Oak mind if we climb it and sleep on a branch?" Del asked.

"Of course not," Crimson replied. "The Old Oak is still a tree after all."

"The Old Oak doesn't glow," Phil observed.

"No, it never has," said Crimson. "Though no light can be observed, once you get to know the Old Oak, you realize that it has an inner light brighter than what most living things could ever contain."

Del wasn't worried about being uncomfortable sleeping on a tree branch. She could have slept on a bag of rocks given her physical and mental exhaustion. They climbed the tree, found some good branches, and drifted off.

*****

When Del awoke, she saw brightly colored birds all around them that had obviously perched there for the night. Crimson was twittering with one of them, which took off as soon as their conversation was complete.

"What was that about?" Del enquired, yawning.

"I've sent a message to a friend, letting him know where we are going, in case…" He trailed off.

"In case we don't make it out. Right?" Phil was awake.

"Well…" Crimson paused. "Well, yes. My friend will come to our aid if we don't send word sometime tomorrow. Now, we had better get up and get going. Breakfast is waiting on the stone down below."

They descended the tree, to find their feast, including some bowl-shaped leaves with glow-water in them. Crimson had already been quite busy that morning, gathering an assortment of berries. They ate and drank. Everything, of course, tasted divine.

After breakfast, the three of them set out. There was no stream to follow this time, and no path. Crimson was their only guide. Without him, they would be doomed.

The day went by uneventfully. They kept silent and moved through the forest swiftly, keeping a faster pace than Crimson had anticipated. It was well before sunset when they arrived at their destination.

"In a few steps, the ground will begin sloping down," Crimson told the children. "There's a well-protected glade, with a thick hedge that runs around it at the bottom of a valley. One side of the glade butts up against a sheer rock wall. We'll need to get closer, and then I'll see if I can talk to one of the nearby trees. Perhaps the diplomatic route can work."

"What do you mean?" asked Phil.

"He's going to try and talk the trees into letting Sam and Guy go," Del explained. "Right?"

"Yes."

"What if that doesn't work?" Phil asked.

"If that doesn't work, we wait until nightfall, and I will sneak into the hedge glade. I will find a weakness and exploit it to get your friends out."

Del was relieved Crimson had a plan B, but Phil still looked concerned.

"Don't worry," Crimson continued. "We will try talking first."

They kept moving. The ground began sloping down, gently at first, then steeper. They entered the valley. Below them, they could see a wall of green, similar to the one that Del and Phil had jumped through to escape the forest the day before. It was the hedge. Del hoped desperately that Sam and Guy were just beyond it. She hoped they were okay and alive. She desperately wanted to see her friends, but especially Sam. She had been way more worried than she had let on.

Del and Phil had gotten some answers from Crimson, but if Sam and Guy had been captured by the trees immediately upon their entry into Azdia, then they had spent more than a day wondering about this terrible place they had come to.

"Okay," Crimson said, signalling for their party to stop. "This is it." Crimson touched the nearest tree, and the rustling, creaking conversation ensued.

"Keep your eyes open, Deli," said Phil. "And get ready to run."

Del felt a little sick, like she needed to throw up. "I don't feel very good," she said.

"Just try to stay focused while Crimson is busy," Phil replied.

Just then Crimson broke off his talk with the tree, and yelled, "No! Run! It's a trap."

*****

Del's berry lunch came spewing out of her mouth. She went down on one knee and heaved a second time.

Phil came to her side, "Del, I know it's bad, but we've got to run."

Crimson turned toward the children and made a choice that solidified their trust in him. Instead of taking off into the forest, he ran toward Del and Phil to try and help them flee.

As Crimson got closer, a second hedge grew up out of nowhere, encircling the three of them. It all happened so fast that, even without Del being sick, they might not have made it out. Within just a few seconds, a fully grown outer hedge was in place. It surrounded them and the inner hedge, within which they were now certain Sam and Guy would be found. They were all trapped by the trees.

"I guess it's plan B," Phil said.

"More like plan C," Crimson replied. "I've got to rescue four of you now, and I don't know if I'm strong enough for that."

For a while, everything was still. Del wanted to ask Crimson what just happened. She wanted to demand an explanation. But she held back, thinking that even the slightest whisper might set the trees off. Crimson held up a hand signalling that they ought to keep silent.

She felt a foreign anger toward the little red-eyed creature welling up inside her. Maybe he was behind all of this. She and Phil had yet to speak to anyone else in this world, and this shape-shifting animal may have been leading them on this whole time. The longer the silence was kept by Crimson's raised hand, the more Del's skin crawled. Ten seconds ago, she was puking her guts out, but now she was feeling strong, and ready to punch out the little wingless fairy.

Crimson let out a breath as though he'd been holding it in the whole time. "I think we can talk now."

As soon as the phrase had left his lips, Del pounced on him, letting fly with punches to his defenceless little body. She tackled him to the ground, pinching, punching, even biting. Anything she could do to hurt him. The whole time she was yelling, "Get us out of here! This is your fault! Get us out of here, fairy! Get us out of here, fairy!"

Phil leapt from where he had been, trying to peel Del off. "Deli! What are you doing?"

Having found some kind of super-human strength, she flipped Phil with ease, almost breaking his arm and back with her toss. Her eyes had turned a putrid shade of green. "Never call me that again!"

Del turned back to face off against Crimson, whose face had a bloody scratch running across it. Standing on a smooth stone, Crimson kicked his shoes off and waited for Del to attack. She raced at him and dove at his chest, but just before she made contact, Crimson transformed himself into a rock. Del crashed into him, bashing her head hard. She lay for a moment motionless on the ground, but that was all the time Crimson needed.

He transformed back into his usual state, grabbed her arm, and quickly became a full grown man, pinning her to the ground. Del thrashed around, but her initial adrenaline rush was wearing off. Her strength was dipping back down to normal levels.

"Are you okay?" Crimson shouted to Phil.

"Ya. I think so."

"Get over here then. She needs you."

Phil raced to Crimson's side.

"Look into her eyes and tell her to remain calm," said Crimson.

Phil didn't know what to do.

"Just do it," said Crimson.

Phil looked at Del. She was looking less and less like herself. She started to foam slightly at the mouth and began twitching uncontrollably. Just then, they heard a muffled voice coming from behind the central hedge.

"Phil! Del! Is that you? Del? Are you... alright?... Phil?"

It was Guy, and at his distant voice, the tiniest spark of light returned to Del's eyes.

"Hurry!" Crimson was urgent now.

Phil searched for the right words to say, then finally blurted out, "We all love you Del! Me, Guy, Sam. Even your mom loves you so much! Don't leave us. Don't ever leave us. We don't know what we would do without you! I don't know what I'd do without you."

Del could not remember the last time she had heard such words and her memory wasn't failing because of her current condition either. It had just been so long since anyone had told her these kinds of things. When she heard them, she knew that Phil had dropped all his defences and was being totally honest and genuine.

On hearing Phil's words, her eyes returned to their natural color and her skin, though pale, got less green in tone. Her breathing began to return to normal. Pain shot out from her side where she had been stung. She didn't let on but simply ran her hand over the bump to check that it was still there. It was tender to her touch.

Crimson let go of his hold on Del, and Phil bent down and hugged his friend.

"I'm sorry," said Phil.

"For what?" Del managed.

"For always calling you Deli."

*****

Guy's muffled voice was still calling out. "Is everything okay? We thought we were never going to see you again. We can't get out!"

"Everything's going to be okay," Phil called back. "We're here to rescue you. We have someone with us who can help. Just hang on. We're going to get you out of there."

Del was recovering, sitting next to Crimson.

"Crimson, I'm sorry," she said. "I don't know what happened. I just felt so angry all of a sudden. I felt like I was... someone else, if that makes any sense."

Crimson looked at her. "It's okay. I didn't know what was happening either, but I knew it wasn't you."

"How did you know what to do?" Phil interjected.

"I didn't, at least not for sure. You see, anytime a lumen or any other creature is sick, words of calm and comfort offered from someone with a deep connection to them is critical for their healing. I took a guess that those words were needed from you. I'm glad I was right, but I've never seen anything quite like this before. I don't know why or how it happened to you."

"I hope it's gone for good," Del said, moving her hand over the bump on her side, feeling the source of her lingering discomfort.

"We do too," said Crimson as he looked toward Del's side, with a puzzled expression.

"We need to save Guy and Sam and get out of here," said Phil. "Crimson, what's your plan?"

"We need to wait until full nightfall, when the trees are asleep," Crimson replied. "It won't be long now. Then, we'll go through the hedge to your friends, get them and all leave together."

"Yes, but how?" said Phil.

"Never mind that now," said Crimson. "Tell your friends to expect us at nightfall and to get some rest. Then you and Del should try and sleep for a bit if you can. I will wake you when it's time."

Neither Del nor Phil were in any mood to argue, and they were both exhausted. Phil communicated the instructions to Guy.

Not having heard Sam's voice yet, Del got up enough strength to go over to the hedge and shout, "Sam, are you there?"

"Ya, I'm here." His voice sounded farther away than Guy's.

That was enough for Del. She knew Sam wouldn't

want to say much without seeing her face to face, so she just left it there.

"Just making sure," she called.

Del and Phil settled in close to one another and, after not too long, fell asleep.

CHAPTER EIGHT

Through the Hedge

Del awoke with a start to find Crimson and Phil standing over her.

"We decided to give you some extra sleep," Crimson said. "You needed a little more rest for what we're about to do."

Crimson held out a leaf bowl full of glowing water. "Drink up."

"Where did you get this?" Del asked.

"You should have seen it," Phil said. "They were these birds, but they had four legs... Well, four arms really. Their main hands were like ours, and they came bringing these bowls of water for us. I wish they'd been big enough to just carry us out of here, but I'll take the water."

"The birds were sent by a friend," said Crimson. "I sent word back with them so he knows we are okay. Now, go on. Drink."

Del took a big swig and instantly felt stronger as sweet liquid passed down her throat. She felt as if it were running even into her fingers and toes. As she shivered with delight at the taste and feeling within her, she tried not to think about the fact that the glow of the water was really tiny glow-bugs. Obviously, Crimson wanted them to drink a lot of it. Maybe the firefly swimmers were really good for them, like some kind of medicine or performance-enhancing substance like the ones that are banned at the Olympics. In any case, Del downed it all and felt much better for it.

"Ready?" Crimson asked.

"We don't even know what we're doing; how can we know if we're ready?" Phil said. Del looked over at him sensing his unease at being kept in the dark about the plan.

Crimson ignored this or didn't pick up on it.

"Let's begin," he said. "Join hands with me."

The children, although very unsure, did as Crimson said.

The glow within Crimson started to grow and become more intense. His grip on the children's fingers tightened to the point that Del thought he would crush her bones. There was no way they would be able to pull back from his hold, and it was a good thing, because, if they had been able to pull away, they most certainly would have considering what happened next.

Crimson's glow intensified until the two brightest spots were passing along both his arms. Del watched as the glow came toward their joined hands. Her heart pounded faster and faster. When the glow reached Crimson's fingers, Del felt a tingling and then a solid heat. She tried to pull away or run but found that she was completely unable to. By the looks of it, Phil was in the same state. The children's hands began glowing like Crimson's, then their arms, then into their chests. The tingling heat followed the pattern of the glow, and all the children could do was watch and feel. What on earth was Crimson doing to them?

Del became hyper aware of her body. She knew things about herself that she hadn't known before. Things that no one ever thinks about, like the exact length of her hair. She could tell where her veins were within her. She could sense her own bones and all her internal organs, their locations, their sizes. It was a terrifying, strange experience. Then, every part of her began to change. Specifically, everything started getting smaller. She looked at Phil, and he was shrinking in every respect as well. Crimson was too, just at a slightly slower rate since he was already half their size. They got smaller and smaller and smaller until the three of them were no larger than the blades of grass. They were perhaps the size of three hummingbirds.

Crimson let go, and the three of them fell to the ground. For all the terror when it was happening to them, the feeling of intense heat, and the weird feeling of her own capillaries and organs, as soon as Crimson let go, Del felt fantastic.

"Wow!" Phil said, clearly feeling the same way. "That was awesome!"

The whole experience had been like going on a terrifying roller coaster: scary and exhilarating. When you get off, you want to get back on again.

"We're going through the hedge!" Del exclaimed. "It's going to be easy."

Crimson lay huffing and puffing. All he could manage was to nod his head. He gave one of his now familiar hand signals that he needed a minute. Clearly what had energized the children had completely wiped him out.

*****

Phil walked over to Crimson and offered him his hand. Crimson grabbed on, and Phil hoisted him back to his feet.

"Let's do it," said Phil.

Crimson, still out of breath, took position in front of the children and led them toward the towering hedge-wall. At this size, they could see all kinds of holes that they could pick their way through. It would be like walking through a dense forest.

Between puffs, Crimson wheezed, "It might take us a while, but, you're right; it shouldn't be too difficult."

The forest of hedge ahead of them had no glow to it. It was much darker than the darkness of night that they were leaving behind. Crimson's inner light still provided a bit of a glow, however, for which they were all very thankful.

They walked, ducking under and hopping over branches, for a long time.

"This hedge is huge!" said Del.

"We're just really small," said Phil.

There was very little to see. The time passed slowly. Del took some consolation in the fact that they were getting closer and closer to seeing Sam and Guy. She had also pieced together the plan in her mind. Somehow Crimson would have to shrink Sam and Guy as well. Then it would simply be a matter of walking through the two hedges to freedom and changing everyone back to normal size. With Crimson's help, she was starting to believe that they would all be able to escape the forest.

Crimson seemed to have fully recovered.

"We need to get a move on," he said. "We still have a lot to do tonight, and this hedge is wider than I thought it would be."

He picked up the pace, half jogging. Del followed, with Phil bringing up the rear.

Del's mind wandered as they ran. She hadn't thought much about home, other than the frequent thoughts of wondering how on earth they would ever figure out how to get back. Now, as she jogged, she could hear Phil's words about her mother loving her ringing in her ears. Her mother would indeed be worried sick.

Before Phil's words had struck Del to the core and pulled her out of whatever sickness had had a hold on her, she couldn't have said that she cared at all about seeing her family again. But jogging through the giant hedge, her mind settled on a memory of a time when she, her mom, and her sister had been truly happy.

They had been on holiday. It was nothing special, just to a campsite about a two hour drive from home. On most nights, different friends of her mom's had dropped by, which had usually been no fun at all. But one night, it had been just the three of them. They had stayed up late roasting marshmallows and eating way too much. They had even sung some silly songs around the campfire. That night, her mom had been more herself than she had been in years. Del remembered wishing that night around the campfire would never end.

At the time, she held such hopes that their lives would be different in the morning, but by the time the holiday was over, they were barely speaking to each other. They had spent the entire drive home plugged into their phones. Things only got worse when they arrived home.

Within a few weeks, her mom was dressing inappropriately and going out on dates like there was no tomorrow. Del often wished she could return to that campfire, but over the last few months, she had slowly taught herself that there was no hope.

Now, lost in a strange world, she realized she missed her mom, and the growing up she had had to do in the last few years helped her know that her mom probably felt the same way about her. Deep down, Del knew what Phil had said was true. Her mother loved her, and her mom would be panicked at her disappearance.

"Phil?" she said.

"Ya?"

"Do you think they're looking for us?"

"Who?"

"Y'know. Our families."

"Probably. Not going to find us though, I don't think, unless the priest and his wife cave and tell them where we are. But I'm not even sure anyone would think to talk to them."

"Aren't you worried that everyone will be... worried?"

"I guess so. But I figure that they're going to think the four of us ran away together. They'll still look for us, but the four of us all gone at the same time, that's what they'll think."

"Do you think they'll stop looking for us?"

"If we take too long getting back, they will. But they'll be in for a shock when we get back, won't they?"

"I'm going to be in so much trouble." Del trailed off as her jog slowed to a walk. "I want to get out of here, and I know my mom's going to be worried and all, but I don't know if I could face her. She'll be too mad."

Del and Phil's pace had slowed to almost nothing, and Crimson's light was moving farther ahead into the darkness.

"It might be easier to just never go back," Del said.

Crimson turned and sprinted back to get them.

"C'mon," he urged. "We can't waste time. Time is not on our side tonight. We must move."

Phil grabbed Del's hand. "C'mon," he said. "Let's go save Guy and Sam."

The three of them took off faster than they had gone before. It wasn't long before they could see the abrupt end of the hedge ahead of them. They broke out into a sprint for the final leg, breaking through into the clearing beyond, eyes peeled. They looked in all directions for their lost and captured companions, but Sam and Guy were nowhere to be seen.

Crimson spun quickly. "Don't say a word. Don't call out. I should have thought about this before, but if they see you small like this they may think something terrible has happened to you. We need to be more cautious."

"Just change us back. Make us big again," said Phil.

"I'm afraid I don't have the strength to metamorph that much. I think I will need to do this alone."

"But..." Del started.

"We can't take the risk." Crimson grabbed her arm and quickly changed into his boy form. "This will be easier for them I think," he said. Letting go of Del's arm, his glow increased the same as when they had shrunk. He gradually got bigger, until he was normal boy-size. Crimson took a quick look around then, puffing and wheezing, stumbled, and slumped down to sit in the grass next to Del and Phil.

"Did you see them?" Del asked, aware that, being

regular size, with his extra height, he was able to see much farther than she and Phil.

Between breaths, Crimson pointed and managed to speak. "They're over there... asleep... near the rock wall... I just need... to catch... my breath."

"Okay - take it easy." Del tried to reassure him. "Just take your time."

They waited together for Crimson to recover from his size change. It was much quicker than when transforming two others along with himself.

"I think I should carry you both over with me, and you can hide somewhere nearby," Crimson said.

"Sounds good," said Del.

Phil nodded.

Crimson picked up the two tiny children and crept toward the place where the others lay.

*****

"I hope they won't be too frightened to meet me," Crimson confessed.

Del thought for a moment. "I'm thinking that so far they've been frightened enough by trees taking them captive. If they're anything like us, and they are, they'll be a little scared - but they'll be more relieved than anything else. Besides, they know we're coming. They'll probably just wonder where Phil and I are."

"I guess so," said Crimson.

Crimson put Phil and Del down beside a small rock they could hide behind that was close enough to watch what was about to take place.

"This should work nicely," said Crimson. "Now, don't wander off. After we change, I'll bring them here to see you."

Del and Phil nodded.

Crimson walked over to the sleeping boys, then looked back in the direction of the rock to see Phil and Del's faces staring at him. Del gave him a thumbs up sign. Phil looked concerned. Crimson opened his mouth to say something, then stopped. He knelt down next to the two boys and once again looked in the direction of Del and Phil.

"What's he waiting for?" Del said to Phil. "Why doesn't he wake them up?"

"I have a bad feeling about this," said Phil.

Suddenly Crimson called to them. "There's no time to explain anything. I'm going to have to do this right now."

"Oh no," said Del. She came out from behind the rock, realizing what Crimson was about to do.

Phil held her back. "There's nothing you can do. Just let him."

The boy-sized Crimson latched onto an arm of each of the sleeping boys. Crimson's deep glow became more chaotic and intense as it moved to his extremities. The glow hit Sam and Guy, and it woke them with a start. Each of them screamed in horror. Del and Phil knew that it wouldn't last long and it would feel exhilarating in a minute, but they also knew what an intense experience the size change was. Imagine waking up as you are pushed out of a plane having no idea if you have a parachute on. Their screams echoed in the forest. Surely this would wake the trees. Del presumed that this is what Crimson was calculating just before taking his drastic action. Was it worth the risk to save the time of having to explain everything to Guy and

Sam?

"We need to be there when they come out of this," said Phil. "Crimson's going to be weak, and they won't know what hit them. Let's go."

He grabbed Del by the hand, and the two of them began running.

Crimson, Sam and Guy were wrapped in light. Crimson looked as though he could barely continue as they shrunk down to miniature size. Sam and Guy kept screaming.

"Did we sound like that?" Del asked.

"I don't think so," said Phil.

"Maybe something's going wrong. It seems to be taking longer."

"And Crimson doesn't look good at all. I think it might be killing him."

Del and Phil continued racing toward the bright chaos. Then it all stopped. Guy and Sam stood there with stunned looks on their faces, and Crimson collapsed in a heap.

"Guys, it's okay," Phil called. "It's us. This is all part of the rescue."

Del didn't know who to run to first. She felt such a strong urge to go to Crimson and make sure he was okay, or alive. But she ran to Sam instead, hugged him, and told him everything was going to be okay.

"That was horrible," Guy exclaimed, "And awesome."

"I know, right?" said Phil.

"We're small!" Sam said.

"You've always been small," joked Phil.

The three boys were back. They pushed each other around playfully, joking with each other back and forth, generally ignoring Del. They easily slipped into their old routine of Guy and Phil acting cool and the younger Sam trying to fit in. They would come around to poking fun at Del any minute.

But Del was kneeling next to Crimson, holding his limp hand. There was no light left in him. All was dark.

Phil noticed them. "Is he going to be okay?"

Del, tears in her eyes, shook her head.

CHAPTER NINE

Reunited

Del and Phil knelt at Crimson's side with Guy and Sam standing a little way off.

"What was that thing, anyway?" Guy asked.

"His name is Crimson," Del shouted, looking daggers at Guy. "He helped us find you. He's the only reason we survived."

"We don't have a lot of time," Phil reminded them. "I'm not sure how the trees didn't wake up with all that screaming, but we don't want to be around here when they do wake up."

Tears streamed down Del's face. "Why did we come to this awful, awful place?"

"And why would this thing sacrifice itself to change us all into tiny little people?" asked Sam.

"He's not a thing," Del protested.

"Sorry, but still. Why would he go through that if it was going to kill him?" Sam persisted.

"Because he believes that we are something that we're not," Del said. "He thinks we're here to save his kind. And we let him believe it, just to make sure he would help us rescue you!'"

"We didn't know this would happen though, Del," said Phil. "Look... we've got to go."

"I'm not leaving him," Del sobbed. "Not like this."

Phil grabbed Del to try and pull her away, but she clung at Crimson's shirt. Phil pulled harder but Del's grip was so tight that two buttons on Crimson's shirt popped off, revealing his chest.

"Look!" said Guy and Sam together. A very faint red light glowed at the centre of his chest.

"He's still alive!" Del proclaimed. "We have to help him."

"Del, say something comforting or whatever to him. Like I did for you," Phil instructed, hurriedly. "Crimson said it worked, and you have the best connection with him out of any of us."

Del bent low, looked into Crimson's dead eyes and said, "Crimson, we're sorry. We're sorry for not telling you the truth. We're just regular kids but we're going to get you out of here now. Everything is going to be okay. We'll find others like you; we'll take you to your home. You just have to keep your light going."

Crimson didn't wake at her words, but the red glow got just a little bit brighter and a little bit bigger.

"Del, it's working," said Phil. He turned to Guy and Sam, who looked skeptical. "We're going to do exactly what Del said. We're taking Crimson with us. No argument."

That settled it for the group. Their leader had spoken, and that's what they would do.

Their saving grace was that Crimson had shrunk himself and had stayed that way, as they all had. Guy and Phil were bigger than him and together they would have no problem carrying Crimson. If Phil ordered it, Guy could probably sling him over his shoulder and do much of the trekking on his own.

Phil took control. "We're not going back the way we came. It's too long to get out of the forest. C'mon Guy. Help me with Crimson; we're heading that way." Phil pointed to where the hedge met the rock wall.

*****

It took some time to reach the junction of the hedge and the rock wall. The rock was a sheer face reaching sky high. Had they been regular size, and without an extra body to carry, they may have contemplated climbing it, but there was no way that was going to happen under current conditions.

They entered the hedge, moving slowly because of their load and because of the increased darkness that lay inside. Without a brighter light from Crimson, the dark was intense. They stayed close to each other so they could at least see each others' silhouettes. They stayed close to the rock wall, feeling their way along it. They only strayed from it when some thick part of the hedge blocked their way. When that happened, their top priority was to find the rock wall again and continue shuffling along it.

This was also their first real opportunity to talk just the four of them. Phil started things off. "What happened to you guys, anyway?"

"It's going to sound crazy," Guy said.

"Have you noticed our size and that we're carrying a little glowing elf?" Phil retorted. "I think we've got plenty of crazy already."

Guy started telling their story. "When we landed in this forest, it was all pretty quiet. We started looking for you guys. No matter how loud we yelled, we got nothing back. We figured you had to be a long way off, somewhere. Then it got really weird. Out of nowhere, the trees attacked us. There were swinging branches. They tried to bat at us with giant leaves. It was insane. We took off - I'm not sure I've ever seen Sammy run so hard in my life. The trees kept blocking us and we kept dodging them. We ran until we got to that place where we just were. There were less trees all of a sudden, and all the chaos stopped. We stopped when we saw this big rock wall in front of us. By the time we'd turned around, there was this hedge, and we were trapped."

"Did you try and get out?" Del asked.

"Of course we did," Guy replied. "But we figured out pretty fast that there was no way we were getting through the hedge. You could kind of squeeze into it a little bit, but it was just way too thick. I tried climbing the hedge too and almost got completely stuck. Sam had to pull me out.

"Climbing the rock wall was just too hard as well. We didn't know what to do, but it seemed like someone was taking care of us, too. After sleeping, fresh berries would show up for us to eat. Every now and again, it rained, and to be honest, the rain tasted better than anything I'd ever tasted before. We knew we were prisoners and there was nothing that could be done. I think Sam was doing a lot of thinking. He would have figured a way out eventually - but then you all came along. What about you guys?"

Del and Phil told their much more involved tale. Guy and Sam listened, amazed, as they heard of the Old

Oak, the tale of Eleanor and, most impressively, their friends' ride atop the feldroes. As their story was recounted, Del thought how much had happened to her and Phil already since arriving in Azdia.

She longed for home, but this was not a time to wallow in any kind of despair. She resolved to be action-oriented instead. She didn't just want a plan for getting out of the forest, but a plan for getting out of the strange and dangerous world in which they were trapped. Her thoughts kept coming back to the priest's poem that she and Phil couldn't quite remember.

"We need to figure out how to get home," she said. "We need to figure out what the priest was talking about right before we left the graveyard."

"The weird poem?" Guy said. "Can't remember a word."

"I can," said Sam. "I think it's a riddle, not a poem. I've been thinking about it a lot. When the priest told us to remember it, I just kept repeating it to myself over and over again. But... I can't figure out what it means."

"Tell it to us Sam," Phil said. "Del and I couldn't quite remember the whole thing."

Sam repeated it.

Carry yourselves beyond the number
Through the place of the tallest lumber.
Seek the one from whom under you slid
Whose name you found when only you hid.
Within this one's fence, the door shall appear.
You won't see if you look, but you will if you hear.

"I get that we are supposed to go 'beyond the number'," Sam continued. "But what exactly is that?"

"I don't know," said Guy. "Phil, d'you think figuring this out'll get us home?"

"It's kind of all we've got right now," said Phil.

Del thought about the number, and then realized that Sam was notorious in their group for asking a question when he had at least a partial theory to explain something. He was almost always on the right track but was usually too nervous to say anything, and preferred to let others take the lead.

"Sam," Del questioned, "Do think you know what 'the number' is?"

"Well... I don't know, really, but it might be, but probably isn't..."

"Just spit it out!" Phil demanded. "Getting home might depend on it, and if you know anything at all, you need to tell us."

"Okay, okay. I was just thinking that the only number that we've seen, that the priest knows we've seen, is the date on the gravestone."

"That's stupid!" said Guy. He was always so encouraging.

"Shut up, Guy," said Phil. "What was the date?"

Sam's voice cracked, "I don't know. I just can't picture it. Sorry guys."

"It's 1875 to 1889," Del said. "I'm one hundred percent sure."

"Wow," said Phil, impressed. "But, even if we know the number, what does it mean to go beyond the number?"

"Beyond 1889 is just 1890, but I don't think that helps us," said Del. "You're the one who's good at riddles, Sam."

Sam, deep in thought, didn't answer.

"Maybe we just need to think some more," said Guy.

"Maybe we need to ask Crimson when he wakes up,"

said Del.

"Hey! I think we might be at the end of the hedge," said Phil, who had been leading the shuffle along the rock wall as they had talked. "Yeah - this is it."

*****

As they exited the hedge, Sam breathed a sigh of relief. "We made it. Thank God."

Phil broke the bad news. "This is just the first hedge. There's another one to go through that you can't see yet. We've got to cross a clearing first."

He didn't wait for the other boys to get dejected. He just kept moving.

While Guy and Sam carried Crimson, Del walked next to Phil and whispered to him, "I think Crimson's plan was to try and get out of the forest tonight. But I'm not even sure we'll make it through the second hedge before the sun comes up."

"We've got to try though, right?" said Phil.

"I guess so," said Del. "I just think maybe we need a backup plan. Maybe we need to look for a place to hide during the day, when the trees are awake."

"What did you have in mind?" Phil asked.

"It might actually be better to stay inside one of the hedges for the day. The problem is, we're not going to last very long without some water. Crimson really needs some."

"Let's just keep going for now," said Phil. "We'll get into the second hedge and see how far we get. We have a few more hours for sure."

As they crossed the clearing, it didn't take long for them to see the hedge looming on the horizon.

"The clearing must be narrower here by the wall," Del remarked.

"Let's hope the hedge is narrower, too," Phil said.

They continued alternating who carried Crimson. They entered the second hedge and, as they walked, there was no talk about getting home, the riddle, or the dates on the gravestone because none of them had a bright idea or a solution. As hoped for, this hedge was much narrower than the first; there was still some night left when they reached the end of it.

"It's decision time," Del said. "Are we still going, or are we hiding in the hedge?"

*****

"We're going," said Phil.

The four friends and Crimson, being carried solely by Guy at this point, continued to follow the rock wall that appeared to be curving slightly. Del couldn't help thinking about how, if only they were bigger, they might be able to scale the wall and get a look at the forest from above. This was clearly impossible at their current size. A breeze seemed to be blowing through the soaring treetops and the darkness was not as thick as it had been. They had found no obvious place to hide. The trees were becoming more active as the children pressed on.

"I think the trees are starting to wake up," said Guy.

"We've got to find somewhere to hide," said Del.

"I think we should try and pick up the pace," said Phil. "Guy, how're you doing carrying our friend?"

"I'm okay." Guy straightened up a little. "I actually think it's easier on my own. I can go faster."

It was not long before they came to a small alcove in the rock wall.

"I think we've got to hide here," said Phil. "We can't risk staying in the open with these trees."

"But what about water?" ask Del. "We have nothing to drink."

"I think we need rest more than water right now anyway," Phil replied. "I'll go out in a little while and search for some if we are in desperate need. We should be okay for now."

The alcove provided the friends with enough cover from the forest to feel safe. They could still see along the rock wall in both directions. As it turned out, this was a very good thing since it was from along the wall that their salvation came.

CHAPTER TEN

The Falls

Coming towards them was a lumen.

At their current small size and under the protection of the alcove in the rock wall, Crimson and the four friends would not be easily seen or heard by the approaching lumen. They would have to work to get noticed.

"Should we talk to him?" Guy whispered.

"Yes," said Del. "I'm sure he will help us, especially if he sees Crimson."

"It's worth a shot," said Phil. "Better than trusting the trees."

"And better than dying of thirst," said Sam.

Del and Phil walked out from the alcove a little bit, keeping one eye on the rustling trees, and one on the towering figure approaching them. He was not looking down. Del tried to think of a way to get his attention without startling him. Phil, however, didn't seem to care about that.

"Hey! You!" he yelled.

Leaves rustled and branches creaked.

"Phil, shhh. The trees," Del said.

Phil ignored her. "Hey! Down here!"

"Phil. Quiet. He's not going to understand you anyway."

The lumen stopped and looked around. He touched a nearby tree trunk, and a rustling sound came out of his mouth.

"He's talking to the trees," Del said.

"Maybe they'll tell him we're here," said Phil. He turned back toward the alcove. "Guy, Sam, you guys stay here and make sure Crimson stays safe. Del and I are going to talk to him."

Del and Phil moved toward the lumen, watchful for a potential tree attack, which fortunately did not come. They got pretty close to him before he finally spotted them. The lumen broke off his conversation with the tree and took several steps toward them. Del and Phil froze. The sight of a strange, giant lumen loping toward them was a frightening one.

He came at them quickly and went down on one knee. His giant hands reached out. Del and Phil stood, transfixed. He grabbed at them and picked them both up easily.

"This may have been a big mistake," said Del.

Phil nodded.

The lumen's eyes glowed a deep blue. He gazed at them, then spoke, "I thought you'd be bigger."

Del started to attempt an explanation, but the lumen spoke again before she could think of what to say.

"Where's Crimson?" said the lumen.

What a relief to hear him say Crimson's name.

"He's small like us," Phil replied. "He saved us but had to turn us all small to do it."

"Both of you?" the lumen asked.

"Yes, and two others," Phil said.

"He turned four of you small, and himself? How big were you to start with?"

"Bigger than Crimson," Del said. "I suppose bigger than you although I can't imagine it right now, as you seem to be a giant."

"That kind of shapeshifting…" the lumen thought out loud, "Crimson must be in terrible condition. That is if he survived at all. Where is he?"

Del and Phil directed the lumen to the alcove. He knelt down and released Del and Phil, who quickly ran toward their friends.

"I think it's going to be okay," said Phil. "I think he's going to help us."

"This won't do at all, not at all," said the giant, peering into the alcove. "We must get you out of here. All of you. I'm going to take you somewhere safe. It will be easier if you stay this size for now."

"It's a bit unnerving, isn't it?" said Sam to his friends. "Being this small, with a giant creature picking us up and all."

One of the giant's hands grabbed Crimson, placed him in one of his pockets then returned to grab Phil.

"Hold on," Phil said. "What's your name? And how did you find us?"

"The name's Hollow, at your service. And I was looking for you because I wasn't too pleased with Crimson's last check-in. He told me he had everything under control, which to me sounded like he was about to do something foolish. Looks like I was right. I knew he would need help, so I came as fast as I could. But now, I need to get you out of here."

He hurriedly swept up the four friends and placed them in a small satchel leaving the top flap open.

"You should be alright in here," he said. "I'll get you all back to normal size as soon as I can."

*****

The giant lumen took off at a jog, and the children bounced around in the satchel. Del and Sam grabbed onto a small strap to steady themselves. Guy tried to balance in a fold of the canvas of the bag, while Phil attempted to tie a loose thread around his arm to hold himself in place.

"This is crazy!" Del shouted.

The others nodded in agreement. They tried hard to look out of the satchel, but with all the bouncing, they couldn't catch a glimpse of anything significant: only stray branches, leaves, and the occasional burst of light. As they travelled, they began to hear a noise. This noise was different than the rustle of leaves or the creaking of branches that had now become so familiar. This noise was constant and getting louder.

"What is that sound?" Phil asked.

"Whatever it is, I think we're heading towards it," Del postulated. "I don't know if that's a good thing or not."

Eventually they gave up trying to talk as their conversation was increasingly drowned out by the sound which had become a deafening and consistent roar.

They stopped abruptly and saw Hollow's fingers on the lip of the satchel. The fingers made an adjustment to the fabric of the bag making it easier for them to look out beyond its brim.

"Thought you might like to see this," Hollow shouted

over the roar.

They were in a clearing. The ground had transformed into mostly rock. The clearing was short on trees and full of mist. The mist, like slow-falling rain, made everything in the immediate area wet, including Hollow's clothes. The children welcomed the mist as it drifted onto their heads and faces. It was refreshing.

Del could see from the top of the satchel into the pocket where Crimson lay. Smiling, she elbowed Phil and pointed at Crimson. His regular glow was returning, as though the moisture had some kind of healing power.

"I knew it," yelled Sam, trying to get his voice heard over the roar. "I knew it."

Del put her ear close to his mouth as though he was going to whisper something to her.

He yelled again. "It's a waterfall!"

Del's eyes widened. She gazed through the mist and, sure enough, she could see veiled water falling rapidly under the high arch of a small rainbow. She wondered at what it might represent, vaguely remembering that rainbows were supposed to be a sign of promise. At present, it represented getting something to drink. They had found water and plenty of it.

Hollow set off again, walking this time, taking deliberate, careful steps over the slippery rocks. They moved closer to the falls, getting wetter and wetter. The four friends tried hard to keep their heads above the edge of the satchel so they could see.

Closely following the rock wall, Hollow passed along a path behind the falls. Streams and streams of water fell from above, down into a pool of mist. The rushing water was full of colored light dancing up and down at an incredible pace, making what would have normally been a very dark place into a beautiful, multi-colored tunnel of light.

Hollow stopped and this time pulled the children out of the satchel. He placed them next to a small pool of water. The water in the pool was fed by the mist and spray, but overflowed back down into the depths. With their small size, the pool was an oasis. They had found their drinking fountain, their source of life.

"We're stopping here for some rest," Hollow announced as he laid Crimson gently beside the pool.

After a good drink, the boys quickly fell asleep as Del helped Hollow pour water into Crimson's mouth. Then she drifted off as well.

*****

It was the best sleep Del had had since arriving in Azdia. When she finally did wake up, she saw Crimson's eyes open. The water had worked. He was okay.

He motioned for her to come nearer, and as he spoke, she listened intently.

"You... have... done... well... Del," he said softly.

Del couldn't hear it, but she read his lips as best she could, since most of his speech was drowned out by the roar of the falls.

That was all he seemed to be able to manage to say in his still weakened condition. He slumped back down, but his eyes remained open and bright.

The others were waking up, too.

Del went over to Phil and yelled, "Crimson's going to be okay."

"He is indeed," Hollow said, emerging from a

shadow a little father back from the falls.

"Come on everyone," Hollow continued. "Get back in your places. You will all be back to normal size soon enough."

He shot Crimson a disapproving but loving look. Crimson just closed his eyes and allowed Hollow to put him back in the pocket. The four friends rode in the satchel and while Hollow walked slowly behind the falls they were able to keep their heads out and look around.

On the other side of the falls, there was a staircase cut into the rock wall leading up. Hollow began the climb, which took some time. Del figured the slow pace was due to the steps being slippery from continual spray from the falls. She welcomed the mist, however. She found that she could breathe it in and be utterly refreshed by its sweet flavor. It was like drinking air, or perhaps more accurately, like breathing in a cool drink on a hot day.

As they neared the top of the stairs, the spray and the roar lessened. The falls were very high, and the farther they were from the bottom where the falls crashed into the rocks below, the less they had to contend with the deafening sound.

The friends could have heard each other had any of them spoken, but they didn't. Instead, as they rose out of the mist, they stared out at the beautiful landscape that unfolded before them. This was far beyond what Del and Phil had seen from the top of the feldroes.

A beautiful sunset or sunrise, Del didn't know which one, was on the horizon, and through the mist they could see not one, but three rainbows below them. The perfect canopy of trees was broken up only by a ribbon, which was surely the river fed by the falls. As peaceful as the forest looked from above, Del was hopeful that, when they reached the top of the staircase, they would no longer have to contend with the hostile trees that they had encountered so far in Azdia.

"Just a few more steps," Hollow said. "Then I'll need a bit of a break. This is not easy carrying five of you... I don't care how small you all are."

"Once we're at the top, we can walk," Phil said.

"But it will take ten times longer to get anywhere," Hollow said. "Besides, once we're at the top, we'll be at the boat in no time. If you all walk at your size, it'll take forever. Not one of Crimson's best ideas, making you small!"

"I heard that!" It was Crimson's voice, a little muffled from inside the pocket.

"Oh, you've decided to join us from your long nap?" Hollow jibed.

"Turning us all small was a stroke of genius, given the circumstances," Crimson continued. "And really, there was no other way."

"It was incredibly risky," Hollow said.

"It was genius all the same," said Crimson.

"You did well, all of you did," Hollow conceded. "Now, we're at the top. Just a little farther to the boat, but first, I need a drink."

Hollow pulled the children and Crimson out of their places. Del took in the sight around her as Hollow lowered them to the ground. They were a little way from the edge of the cliff. The river next to them raced away over the edge in one direction and stretched toward another forest in the other. She was not looking forward to spending any more time among attacking trees. Just on the edge of the tree line, she saw what looked like the mast of a sailboat.

"Is that the boat you're talking about?" Del asked.

"Sure is," said Hollow. He pulled a cup from another pocket, bent down and dipped it in the rushing water. He drank it and repeated the process several times. "Won't take long to get there. Then, we'll be safe."

CHAPTER ELEVEN

Hollow's Boat

As promised, they arrived at the boat in very little time. It was docked at a pier in a small lagoon that edged the tree line of the forest: a last stop before the falls for any boats that might be navigating the river. The river was wide and, judging by the size of the boat, Del figured it must be deep as well. The boat had one central mast with holes along the sides of the hull, almost certainly for oars. It looked as though the boat was built to hold cargo, and some large cargo at that.

Hollow went aboard and emptied the children out of the satchel and Crimson out of his pocket. Two other lumens were on the main deck. Del imagined they must be some sort of crew for the boat. They seemed unfazed by the presence of the tiny children and the tiny Crimson.

"Welcome aboard the Zephyr," Hollow said. "Now, first things first. Let's get you all back to the right size."

"Won't that kill him?" Guy said looking at Crimson, who was still quite weak.

"Not in the slightest," Hollow replied. "At least not if

he lets us do it and doesn't try to change four separate objects at one time by himself, like he did before."

"It wasn't all at the same time," said Crimson, looking a little sheepish, "It was two, then two later in one night."

"And with no food or water!" Hollow laughed. "Crazy Crimson! You're lucky your friends here helped you."

"Excuse me," Del said. "He's the one who rescued us, several times."

"Yes, I'm sure he did, but there isn't any way he would be alive and in such good health, after what he did, unless someone had applied some medical treatment."

"We didn't do anything," Del said. "We just carried him out."

"I'm sorry to disagree, my dear," said Hollow. "But someone spoke words to him, and pretty powerful ones at that."

"Oh… yeah…" Del struggled to say anything in return as she realized that her words may have saved Crimson's life.

"I see that it was you. Crimson and I are in your debt." Hollow bent down on one knee, took Del's tiny hand, and kissed it. "You are indeed a lady."

The thought of Del being a lady was too much for Guy. He burst out laughing and the other boys followed suit.

"Shut up! Idiots!" Del ran over to Guy and punched him in the arm. Phil sat back and smiled.

"And what are you smiling at?" Del threatened.

"It's just nice to have us all together and back to our old selves," said Phil. "Well, almost our old selves."

"Like I said - let's get you back to the right size," Hollow interrupted. He chirped to the other two lumens, who had been busy on the other side of the deck. They scurried over to the group.

"Everyone - this is Verdi and Egreck," Hollow continued. "The best crew you will find anywhere in Azdia. Now join hands all of you - and make sure there is a lumen between every visitor."

They made a circle alternating lumens and tiny kids. The three healthy lumens began to glow more intensely, and each child felt an unyielding grip. Within a few moments, they were back to their regular size. The kids were exhilarated by the transformation, but the lumens, including Crimson, were of course, drained.

"Come to the table," Hollow said between heavy breaths. "Verdi and Egreck have prepared quite a spread for us."

*****

Walking over to where the other two lumen crew members had been doing their work, Del saw a magnificently set table right there on the main deck of the boat. There must have been enough food to feed them all for a week. The most plentiful food was by far berries, but there were other things too: fresh buns, cheeses, fish of several kinds, and what looked like lobster or crab.

"This is the best we can do on short notice. I'm sorry it can't be more." Hollow apologized.

Del wondered at what he was talking about. How did lumens usually eat?

"Nonsense," Crimson said. "This will be fine to give

us some energy."

They all sat down. Hollow was at the head of the table, Crimson next to him, the children in the middle, then Verdi and Egreck at the foot. Guy grabbed a nearby bun and tore it open with his teeth. Hollow looked a touch taken aback.

"We don't eat without toasting the one who has made all of this possible," Hollow said.

The children looked blankly at Hollow, then Crimson.

"I thought being who you are, you'd know all about him." Hollow seemed perplexed.

"Being who we are?" Guy wondered out loud, as Phil kicked him under the table.

"I figure the Malak ought to know who Mr. Thicket is."

"We're not the Malak," Del blurted out suddenly.

Phil looked horrified.

"Well, we're not," Del continued. "And Crimson is entitled to the truth. We're just kids. We don't know anything, and we can't help you save Azdia."

Crimson and Hollow smiled at each other.

"We know you're children," Crimson said. "And I know that you don't believe you are the Malak yet."

"Hmm. I never expected the Malak to not know who they are, and to not know about Mr. Thicket," said Hollow. "What an interesting turn of events."

"So, you're not mad?" said Phil.

"Mad?" Crimson chuckled. "Of course not. You have been sent here, whether you believe it or not, to stop the return of the growing darkness. You being here is a sign of great hope. How can we be mad?"

"But, what if you're wrong?" said Sam.

"We're not," said Hollow. "But, even if we are, then we've met four new friends and had an adventure with them."

"But Crimson almost died back there," Del said.

"Most commendable, yes, but not surprising, when you know Crimson. I might tease him for being foolish, but the truth is that Crimson or I, and many other lumens, would lay down our lives for our friends, especially new friends like you."

The children were dumbfounded at this, and they sat in silence for a while.

Hollow broke in again. "Now, since you don't seem to know anything and don't believe you are who you really are, we will start with the toast itself. Not because it is the best place to begin, but because I'm hungry and we can do plenty of more talking while we eat. So pick up your glasses, hold them high, and repeat after me, in a nice loud voice."

The children and the lumens, including the two silent ones at the end of the table, raised their glasses.

Hollow proudly proclaimed in a loud voice: "To Mr. Thicket!"

Everyone repeated in unison and with gusto, "To Mr. Thicket!"

Del even heard some chirps from the far end of the table. The other two were not mute after all. She glanced over at them, wondering.

"Don't mind them," Hollow said. "They're just quiet. But you couldn't ask for a better crew. Now dive in."

The children helped themselves to mountains of bread, cheese, berries and fish, and it was all fantastic. Del had never tasted anything like it. Everything that she put in her mouth was scrumptious.

"They don't know who they are…" Hollow spoke up again, looking at Crimson. "So, what's our plan, then?"

Before Crimson could respond, Del jumped in, "We need to get home. I know you want us to be the Malak for you, but we're from… somewhere else… and we need to get back there. Our plan needs to be for us to get home."

"I see," said Hollow. "Then, that's our goal. Our good lady has spoken. We will do everything in our power to get you home."

Crimson looked at Hollow, "Are you sure? We need them."

"If they are the Malak, then whatever desire is greatest in their hearts ought to be what we follow."

"So far, so good," said Guy through a mouthful of food. "My greatest desire was for cheese!"

"We don't know how to get them home," said Crimson.

"Then we find someone who does," said Hollow.

Del poked Sam in the ribs and glared at him, silently urging him to speak up. He looked at Del, hesitating.

Then he spoke, timidly. "We were given a riddle before coming here. Part of it tells us to go beyond a number."

"What number?" Hollow asked.

"Go on," Del said.

"We think maybe, one number past 1889, so 1890." Sam said. "Does that mean anything?"

"Do you think it might be part of an address?" Crimson asked.

"Maybe," said Hollow. "Where did you learn of this number?"

"We saw it on a grave," Del said.

"A grave? That doesn't make any sense," said Hollow.

"Maybe we just need to head to the eighteenth province," said Crimson.

"I don't think there are those many towns in eighteen, though," said Hollow.

"Excuse me," said Phil. "What are you talking about?"

"Azdia has eighteen provinces, and they all have a number," Crimson explained. "Every town in every district has a number as well. Your number is 1889, so that would mean province 18, town 89. The problem is, there aren't are 89 towns in the eighteenth province; at least, we don't think there are."

"You don't know for sure?" Phil asked.

"No, not definitively," said Hollow. "Most provinces only have ten or twelve towns. Some of them only have four or five. It's pretty easy to keep them straight. Eighteen is harder though. It is the largest province, and we don't know it that well. I always thought there were around seventy towns. I'd be shocked if there were almost ninety."

"If you don't know for sure, maybe we should just go there like Crimson said," Phil suggested.

"Perhaps," said Hollow. "But we need to have some degree of certainty before we set off."

"You said there was a riddle?" Crimson asked.

"Yeah," said Sam.

"Tell him," said Phil.

Sam repeated the riddle

Carry yourselves beyond the number
Through the place of the tallest lumber.
Seek the one from whom under you slid
Whose name you found when only you hid.

Within this one's fence the door shall appear
You won't see if you look, but you will if you hear.

"Does this mean anything to either of you?" Del asked Crimson and Hollow.

They shook their heads.

"What about the other number?" said Guy. He had finally taken a breath in between wolfing down handfuls of cheese and fruit.

"What did you say?" asked Hollow.

"The other number. Does it mean anything?"

"What other number?" asked Hollow, turning to Sam and Del.

"Well, on every gravestone there are two years, two numbers," said Del.

"I figured if we are going beyond the number, like the riddle says, we needed to use the last number, the largest one," said Sam.

"I think sometimes you just think too much," said Guy.

"What's the other number?" Hollow asked.

"1875," said Del.

Hollow ran over to a cupboard and pulled out a piece of paper and what looked like a pencil. He brought it over and placed it in front of Del.

"Write down everything that was on that gravestone," he ordered.

Del wrote and then showed it to Crimson and Hollow.

BLYTHE

1875 - 1889

"That's an address!" Crimson cried. "That's exactly how we write addresses in Azdia. The first part is the province and the town. Province eighteen. Town seventy five. The second part is the house number. That address is house number 1889 in town 75 in province 18. We need to go to that address."

"Beyond that address," said Sam.

"What's that word?" asked Hollow, pointing at the paper.

"Blythe," said Del. "Do you know who that is?"

"No," Crimson said, "But if we go to that address maybe we'll find out.

"We leave tonight for the eighteenth province," said Hollow.

"Is it far?" Sam asked.

"It's not a short trip," said Hollow. "The fastest way is to cross the Great Lake, which makes up most of the fourteenth province."

"How long will it take?" asked Del.

"We won't be there tomorrow, but we will be sometime after that," Hollow replied.

"So, two days?"

Hollow and Crimson each gave her confused looks as though the question was complicated.

"Sometime after tomorrow," Hollow repeated.

"So, how many days will it take?" Del asked again.

"Sorry, my dear, I'm not quite sure what you are asking," Hollow said.

"I'm asking how long it will take to get there!"

"And I've answered. After tomorrow," Hollow said firmly. "Now, perhaps you all need some rest, my friends. Crimson, Egreck, Verdi and I will take care of everything. Crimson, why don't you show them to some sleeping quarters."

Crimson opened up a door to a small wooden ladder leading below deck and signalled for the children to follow. He led them to two rooms: one small one for Del, and another one with four bunks for the boys and Crimson to share. Del, welcoming the break she was about to get from the others, said a quick goodnight, went into her room, and closed the door behind her.

CHAPTER TWELVE

Voyage On The Lake

This was the first time Del had been alone since arriving in Azdia. She breathed deeply and sighed. As much as she loved her friends and was beginning to love being around Crimson and Hollow, when the door closed behind her, she felt a weight lift. Alone she could be completely herself. No pretending.

The room had a bunk bed. Del would have normally leaped up onto the top bunk, but she was more exhausted than she should have been. Her hand moved to her side and slid over the bump that had formed where she had been stung. It hurt.

She sat down on the lower bunk and sighed. She heard a very similar sigh echo from under the covers. Del's head swung around to see the covers moving. Something was in her bed. She let out a little peep, not a yell by any means, and jumped away from the bunk. As she did, she heard a little peep matching hers.

"What's in there?" she said nervously to herself.

A response came back: not words, but three sounds mimicking her three syllable sentence.

The moving lump under the sheets was not very big, but it was big enough: about the size of a cat or a rabbit. She moved cautiously back toward the bunk and grabbed the edge of the sheets. Del took a deep breath and braced herself. She peeled the sheets back slowly. There was no change in the small movements of the lump. Then she went for it. She flung the sheets back and threw them to the foot of the bed. A white ball of fur scurried quickly toward her pillow clearly seeking cover from a potential attack.

"You're cute," Del said as she moved a little closer to it.

The animal seemed to calm down a bit and again mimicked Del's voice with its tone. Del thought it looked a little like a cat but more fuzzy than any cats she'd seen. She held her hand out to it and waited for it to make the next move. It moved a little closer, bringing its nose to smell Del's fingertips.

Del smiled and said, "It's okay. I'm not going to hurt you."

Every syllable of Del's speech was mimicked by the fuzzy creature. It started licking Del's hand. She reached over with her other hand and petted it. As she touched the creature, it started changing color. Within seconds, the white fuzzy animal was almost entirely pink.

"Wow," Del said out loud.

The animal repeated the tone and drew closer to Del.

"I guess I'm not going to be alone tonight after all."

She picked it up and snuggled with it for a bit. She had never felt anything softer. The animal's color changed again, to a kind of purple, responding to the affection Del gave.

Just then the boat jolted, then rocked a little bit.

"I guess we just set off for the eighteenth province."

Laying the creature back down on the bed, Del spoke to it. "I think we'd better take a look at my side and see if it's getting any better. You're not going to tell anybody about it, right?"

As if the creature understood, or maybe because there were too many words in the sentence, it looked at Del and just made one long purring sigh.

"I think we're on the same page," said Del.

She took off her sweater and lifted her shirt. Her side had gotten much worse. The center of the sting was a dark green. A green bruising spread out from the centre and wrapped around her onto her back and tummy. The fuzzy creature hid from the sight of it.

"I know, it looks bad," said Del. "It hurts too. But, my mom used to say that bruises usually look worse for a few days before they get better. I'm sure I'm going to be okay."

The creature looked at Del and made a questioning sound. Its fur began turning a more red color than purple.

"I know, I know. I should tell someone. But, they'll just worry, and they'll treat me like a baby. If I was really one of the guys, they'd just tell me to tough it out. So that's what I'm going to do. It'll get better."

She looked down at the red ball of fur.

"It will," she insisted.

Del gathered up the sheets from the foot of the bed, lay down and covered herself. She felt the fuzzy creature curl up to her. She held it affectionately. It was purple again. Del craned her neck to blow out the candles next to her bed, the only source of light in the room.

Lying there, Del could feel the rhythm of the boat's movements, rocking the two of them to sleep.

"We're going to be okay, right?" she asked.

As Del drifted off to sleep, the fuzzy creature purred softly; Del took that as a yes.

*****

A bang came at the door to the room where Del was sleeping. She groggily reached from her bunk, turned the handle of the door, and opened it a crack.

"What is it?" she said.

"Wow - you look terrible," said Sam, observing her completely disheveled hair. "I think you'd better get up - we've let you sleep long enough."

"Is it late?" Del mumbled.

"Uh… ya. You've been asleep for hours."

"Why didn't you wake me up?"

"Crimson said to let you sleep."

"That was dumb. Give me a sec."

Del closed the door, put on her sweater, flattened her hair a bit with her hands, and emerged into the main hallway of the ship.

"Okay, I'm ready."

"What's that?" Sam asked.

Del was holding the fuzzy creature in her hand. It was purple, but at Sam's voice, it began turning red.

"This was in my room last night," Del said. "Look, it changes color. I can make it change to purple by being nice to it. Cool, huh?"

"I guess so," said Sam. He wasn't much for pets.

Together, Sam and Del headed up to the main deck of the boat. The sun shone brightly overhead and it took Del a few seconds to adjust to the light. Crimson, Phil, and Guy were sitting together, talking and laughing away. Hollow was up at the ship's wheel, with a short telescope in his hand. Del's eyes followed the outstretched sail from bottom to top to see Egreck perched atop of it in the crow's nest with a much larger telescope. She looked around and realized that there was no land in sight.

"Where are we?" Del asked.

"While you four were sleeping, we sailed along the river, leaving the forest behind," Crimson explained.

"We were just moving from the river to this lake when I got up," said Sam. "That was about two hours ago I would guess."

"Hey, what's that thing?" Phil said, seeing the fuzzy creature.

"I wondered where you'd gotten to," said Crimson talking to the creature in Del's arms. "She seems to have taken a liking to you, Del, judging by her color."

"It's a she?" Del asked.

"Yes," Crimson replied. "Her name is Tabby. She's a winx."

"She changes color," Del said.

"Her color will start by matching how you feel toward her, and then will display how she feels. Purple is when she really likes something. She really likes you. She usually starts by mimicking sounds. Not in words, but in her own way. Then she'll start responding to you."

"Ya - that happened last night," Del said. "It was like we could talk to each other. Can she understand what I'm saying?"

"Not exactly, but she can quickly understand your mood and your feelings," said Crimson. "All winxes can."

"She's pretty awesome," said Del. "Is she yours?"

"Winxes don't belong to anyone. They aren't pets," Crimson said. "But lumens help take care of them. We wouldn't usually have them on a boat, but Tabby was particularly attached to Verdi, so we made an exception. Seems like she's made a new friend, though. Don't worry, Del. Verdi won't mind."

"Verdi, really?" said Guy. "Doesn't seem like the type to like something so… fuzzy."

"No, I supposed that might seem a little strange to you," Crimson replied. "But looks can be deceiving, can't they, Del?"

"I guess so," Del said.

She wondered whether Crimson knew about her side but tried to put that idea out of her mind.

"I know I asked yesterday," she continued. "But do we know how long it's going to take us to get to eighteen?"

"Yes," Crimson said. "Not tomorrow, but sometime after that."

Del had been frustrated the first time she heard this answer. It was like being on a long road trip and asking "are we there yet?" Mom would always say "not long now." Del wanted something more precise. Here, aboard the Zephyr, it seemed neither Crimson nor Hollow were willing or able to be exact.

*****

Time on board passed slowly at first, Del being preoccupied with the idea of when they would arrive at their destination. She wasn't sure if time was only difficult to keep of track of on Hollow's boat or if it was just part of being in Azdia. Sometimes it seemed like they had been sailing on the great lake for just a day or two. Other times, Del was sure it must have been weeks. They slept only when they got tired regardless of whether it was light or dark. Sometimes it seemed like they got tired in no time at all, and other times they seemed to just keep going and going with no sleep.

Every time one of the children asked how long it would be until they reached their destination, the answer would be the same: "Not tomorrow, but sometime after that."

Del concluded that lumens had very limited ways of talking about time. She noticed that neither Crimson nor Hollow would ever refer to a time of day. There were no clocks. They would never estimate how long something would take by referring to a number of minutes. Most things would take "not too long." It would have been a shock to hear either of the lumens say that they didn't have the time to do a particular activity.

All of this was a little bit strange, but also really nice. There was no urgency even though their mission to get to the eighteenth province was very important.

One of their most leisurely activities was eating. They feasted regularly, and there was always more than enough. Before each meal, they toasted Mr. Thicket. They took time to remember that he was the protector of Azdia. Hollow and Crimson always seemed to talk as though their success depended as much on Mr. Thicket's protection as it did on their own work. They spoke of Mr. Thicket watching over them on the waters. They asked for his guidance to find land.

On the boat, Del learned an important lesson. Just because something is important, it doesn't mean that it ought to be rushed into. Their meals were an illustration of this. They could have used the meal time to push forward along the lake, but eating together and thanking Mr. Thicket were important. More important than reaching their destination quickly.

After learning this lesson, Del stopped asking when they would arrive. Instead she began enjoying her time on board. She bonded with Tabby. She checked her wound whenever she was in private, and it seemed to be getting progressively better.

Del did think about her family, but given the choice, she may very well have chosen to live on Hollow's boat forever.

Once Del shifted her thoughts away from how long it was taking to cross the lake toward enjoying life on the boat, it was as though time sped up. She had only just begun enjoying herself and had only just begun falling in love with Azdia and its creatures when, upon awaking one morning, Hollow announced that the next day they would land.

Egreck had camped out in the crow's nest to stay on the lookout for the first sight of land as the Zephyr sailed on. Before land was spotted, however, Egreck chirped urgently from above. It turned out that he had spotted another ship. Crimson and Hollow took this as good news, and Hollow ordered that they head directly toward it.

CHAPTER THIRTEEN

Dark Storm

The oncoming vessel had three masts and was much larger than Hollow's boat. As they approached, Hollow sounded a bell. The larger ship responded with a loud horn. The two vessels came up alongside one another, and several lumens appeared, looking over the edge of the larger ship. One of them, who looked like he might be the captain, chirped. Hollow responded. The two of them chirped back and forth for several minutes. The children had gathered near Crimson so he could act as a translator for them.

"What's going on?" Phil asked.

"They are fleeing the eighteenth province," said Crimson. "Their captain is explaining that dark times have come upon them, and many have decided to leave and look for a better life in one of the other provinces."

Crimson listened again to the chirping between the two captains. "He's warning us not to go to eighteen," Crimson continued. "He is calling it cursed."

"But we must go," said Phil. "It's all we've got to go on to find our way home."

"I'll tell them," said Crimson, and he chirped into their conversation.

Before long, Hollow walked over to them to provide a report.

"It sounds as if heading into eighteen will be difficult," Hollow began. "But I believe we are up to the task. According to their captain, the province is becoming increasingly dark. He recommends that Tabby does not go there, and I think he's right. A darkening province is no place for a winx. They think most of their winxes have already gotten out of their province, and they have several on board. Tabby would be better going with them."

Del's heart sank just a little. She had grown attached to Tabby over their time on board and would be sad to see her go.

"Tabby won't go alone, however," said Hollow. "Verdi will accompany her."

All of the children were much more sad to see Tabby go than they were Verdi. Verdi seemed annoyed that he would have to leave with Tabby and wouldn't be completing the mission for which they had set out. Hollow, however, was in complete control.

"They have also given us directions to the seventy-fifth town," Hollow said. "We have a heading so that we will land at the right beach. The beach we are looking for is marked with an old stone statue. He says we can't miss it because the old statue is very large. From that beach, there is a marked road that heads north. That road will lead us directly to the town we seek. They gave us this information, but also warned us not to go through with our mission. They believe their home has been lost to the darkness, and that going into that darkness is too dangerous. What do you want to do?"

"We must continue on," said Phil. Del, Guy and Sam all nodded in agreement.

"Then it's settled," said Hollow. "We must get moving."

They said their goodbyes to Verdi and Tabby. A rope bridge was temporarily attached between the two vessels for them to go across. Tabby turned a blue color when Del said goodbye which mirrored Del's feelings exactly. As soon as they were across, the rope bridge was taken back, and the larger ship began pulling away. Hollow moved back to the steering wheel and set his new heading. They set off.

*****

Egreck chirped from the crow's nest. "There's land ahead," Hollow translated for the children.

"But storm clouds, too, I think," said Phil, gazing along their heading.

Egreck slid down the mast. Hollow looked through his scope. "Very thick clouds moving over the land."

"The wind is shifting," said Crimson.

"Pull the sail in," ordered Hollow. "There's a storm coming."

Egreck, aided by Crimson, went to work on the sail as the wind picked up.

"We're going to need your help," Hollow said to the children. "Get below and start rowing."

The children looked at each other, not quite knowing what to do. Guy and Phil had been canoeing before, but that was about the extent of their experience with boats. Sam had been on a Caribbean cruise with his family, but that couldn't count as experience with seafaring. Rather than do as Hollow commanded, the four of them just stood there, glued in place as they watched Crimson and Egreck working against the wind with the sail. By the time the sail was collected, the wind was full on, pushing the boat away from the shore. The clouds had rapidly made their way to the boat and a few drops of rain began falling on the deck.

Crimson and Egreck hurried the children down into the belly of the ship. Egreck grabbed Del's arm. His hands were cold and calloused. Del shuddered at his touch.

"You need to paddle. Now," Egreck said.

There were benches with four large oars at the ready. Egreck pushed Del and Guy onto one bench and gave them a single oar. Sam and Phil got the next one. He and Crimson each had their own. Egreck shouted one word commands to keep them in time, as they needed to paddle together. At first their movements were uncoordinated and sloppy, but Egreck's commands got them into a rhythm. They began working together as a team, pulling as hard as they could.

Darkness fell outside as the storm grew until the only light below deck was the glow from Crimson and Egreck accompanied by the occasional flash of lightning. The sound of the rain pounded over their heads as the waves crashed into the sides of the boat. The storm tossed the small vessel back and forth more and more violently. They were at its mercy.

Egreck tried to direct the children in battling the storm, but none of them were sure that their rowing was doing any good. Waves of trepidation washed over Del with each crash against the boat. She gripped her oar tightly and looked around at her friends. They all looked terrified as well.

A giant crack was heard above them, and a flood of water flew down the stairs. The rowing crew sat in ankle deep water. A bell sounded. Egreck stood up and gave his paddle to Crimson who from then on had to manage two.

As Egreck dashed up the stairs, he shouted, "Keep paddling!"

More crashes from above, more water below; it rose to the children's knees, with debris from the boat floating around them.

"We can't keep going like this! We're all going to die. The ship is sinking!" Sam shouted, and for once, Phil and Guy nodded in agreement, not once accusing Sam of being too weak. They were all gripped with the same terror.

"The Zephyr is the best ship in Azdia. She'll hold together," said Crimson. "She can take on a lot of water and still stay afloat."

"What happened to Egreck?" shouted Del.

"I'll go check," said Phil.

"No," said Crimson. "We're all safer here below, even in knee deep water, than we will be on the deck."

They stopped paddling. All attempts to continue were useless as the boat continued to be thrown around like a rag doll.

"Everyone, grab onto something, and do not let go," Crimson ordered. "And stay close to each other."

The children did as Crimson said. There was another deafening bang from above, accompanied by a great flash of light. The children screamed as the boat began listing to one side.

"That was lightning striking the ship," said Crimson.

"What!" shouted Del. "What about Hollow and Egreck?"

Huge amounts of water were pouring into the boat.

"We're going to sink for sure!" Guy cried.

"Just hang on," said Crimson.

They hung on for what seemed like hours as the boat was beaten by the storm. Neither Egreck nor Hollow appeared below deck. The violence of the storm did not die down. The Zephyr took on water, but as Crimson promised, it held up, at first.

Eventually, the storm found a way, however. A great wave pushed the boat up and dashed it onto a rock. The hull split open, and the great timbers of the boat shattered in all directions.

"Hang onto something," Crimson cried. "Do not give up! Do not give up!"

Wood from the boat flew everywhere; water foamed and roared around them. The friends all lost contact with each other. Del heard the screams of her friends just before the dark water engulfed her. She went under. In all the chaos, though, she never let go of the log that had been one of the main supports for the boat.

In one fell swoop, the boat had been destroyed. The Zephyr was no more. It became a mess of floating debris, adrift in the turbulent storm.

The log to which Del clung floated up to the surface. Her head popped out of the water, and she took a quick deep breath. She could see Crimson's glow under the surface. He was not holding anything. The glow descended into the depths, until it completely disappeared. Crimson had sunk. Del had no idea where Phil, Guy, and Sam were, and there was no sign at all of

Egreck or Hollow. All was lost.

Panic set in. Del could feel a pressure building in her chest, and the pain in her side seared despite the frigid water. All Del could do was hold on. As the waves tossed her about, she caught glimpses of rock around her. They were close to land. Maybe she could get to shore. She tried kicking hard, reluctant to let go of the log, but got nowhere. All she could think was that this was the end. Her friends could all be dead, Crimson had sunk already, her side was killing her; she wouldn't last much longer.

After her panic and anxiety, Del experienced a complete loss of hope. Completely alone, she wept. The storm raged around her, and all she wanted was for it to stop. She thought about how her mom had probably already given up hope of ever seeing her again and how it would be so much easier to just let the storm take her.

She lost all ability to keep fighting. She stopped kicking, took a breath, let go of the log, and let herself go under the water. As she sunk, all was cold and calm. She left the roar of the surface behind and joined the serenity below. She didn't like the idea of drowning, but as she dropped below the storm, she fell in love with the idea of falling asleep in the water and never waking up. She hoped desperately that she would pass out from the cold before she had to start sucking in the water.

She felt bad about giving up, but she was just so tired, and couldn't imagine fighting anymore without her friends. As she descended, however, her survival instinct started to override her hopelessness. She got scared. What had she done? Why had she let go of the log and let herself go under? She frantically tried swimming back to the surface, but she had descended too far.

All was watery and black. This was not the glow-water that they usually drank. Del imagined that if it had been, it would have somehow sustained her or lifted her. But this water was dark and freezing.

Then, out of the corner of her eye, Del saw a red glow below her. What was it? It was hurtling towards her. It glowed red all throughout its body, so Del could see it clearly as it came toward her. It had fins like a fish, but had a lizard-like head and great claws instead of lower fins. If Del had named it, she would have called it a dragonfish. She was transfixed by it as she descended and as it throttled through the water toward her.

It flew through the water, its fins moving like the wings of a great bird. It came straight to Del, reached out with one of its claws and caught hold of her. Del had never imagined anything being able to move through water that fast. It pulled her quickly to a place where the storm seemed less severe. Perhaps it was a natural harbour or something. The dragonfish placed her on the shore and looked at her with its lizard eyes. They gleamed at her, and a small smile came across the creature's mouth.

"Crimson, is that you?" Del said.

No answer came, and the creature disappeared into the deep. Del scrambled up and away from the water. She lay shivering on the smooth pebbles of a beach. The red glow of the dragonfish appeared again, and Sam was deposited on the shore. Del found the strength to run down to him and help him out of the water. The dragonfish brought Guy, then Phil, then disappeared again. The four friends lay together on the pebbles in shock.

"What are we going to do?" said Guy.

The others just lay there in silence for a while.

Del's hope returned as she said, "I think that dragonfish thing is Crimson."

The dragonfish returned on its own this time, and it transformed back into its normal lumen form. Del was right. Crimson ran up out of the water to the children.

"I couldn't find them," he said. Pink tears flowed down his already wet face. "Hollow and Egreck are gone."

Del grabbed hold of Crimson and held him tight. She didn't know what to say but knew he likely needed to hear something. "I'm so sorry," was all she could think of. They sat together on the pebbles, Del's arm draped around Crimson's shoulder.

*****

Crimson and the four friends sat on the beach, shivering. Rain pelted them, and the howling wind did not let up.

"We can't stay here," said Phil. "We've got to find some shelter from this storm. Hopefully, we can wait for it to pass or lighten up a little. Then we can figure out how to find the town."

No one moved.

Phil stood and reached his hand out to Crimson. "I'm sorry. We're all feeling their loss, but they'd want us to keep going."

Crimson grabbed Phil's hand, and the boy helped the lumen to his feet.

"Phil's right," Crimson said. "We need to find a place out of this rain."

The five of them moved as a group up and farther

away from the water, looking in the dark for anything that might give them respite from the storm. The plant life near the water was non-existent; the ground was all pebbles and rock. They moved up an incline away from the raging lake and found a small cave cut into the rock. They holed up there and waited.

The friends had been dealt a terrible blow by the storm, losing the boat and its cargo, but most of all, losing Hollow and Egeck. Hollow had spoken about how any good lumen would sacrifice himself for his friends, particularly new friends, but Del never thought it would actually happen.

Eventually, the heavy rain turned to a drizzle and the wind died to a breeze. The clouds remained, but darkness no longer reigned. They emerged from the cave. Below them, on the pebble beach was some wreckage from the ship. After searching through to find any possible provisions, they walked away with two packs filled with bread, fruit, and cheese and three bottles that they could fill from the lake.

"If we follow the shore, we should still be able to find the beach with the statue," Phil said. "Might take a while, but at least we'll have plenty to drink."

"It may not take as long as we think," Crimson said. "Hollow was heading straight for that beach when we spotted land. He would have done everything he could to get us as close as possible."

It turned out that Crimson was right. They arrived at the beach with the statue before they needed a break. Hollow had navigated superbly but had paid the ultimate price. Del still couldn't believe it.

The statue could not be missed. It was a woman holding what looked like a rock high in the air. Her gaze was fixed out to the sea. She was young and beautiful with flowing hair. The statue was massive, about five times the size of an actual adult woman. The sand of the beach covered the lower half of the statue. Either the statue had sunk or the sand of the beach had built up over the years.

They stood for a few moments admiring her.

"Eleanor," whispered Crimson.

Del half expected the statue to answer to her name being whispered.

They were all reeling from the loss of Hollow and Egreck, but something grew within Del that she couldn't yet explain. She still did not believe that she was a Malak, but she began to accept that Hollow and Egreck had died so that they could reach these shores. What grew within Del was the tiniest grain of hope and the power to believe.

*****

They split up and searched the beach for any sign of a path that might be the one they needed to take.

Not long into their search, Guy called out, "Over here!"

The others ran over to Guy.

"I think this is it," Guy said. He pointed to a small sign that made the shape of an arrow. Etched onto the sign was 1875.

They filled their bottles full and made a plan to ration their food, not knowing how long they would need to tap into the provisions. They started the next leg of their journey. They didn't stop for any breaks. They just kept moving, determined to find the seventy-fifth town of the eighteenth province before the day was done.

Light was beginning to fade as the first buildings of the town appeared on the horizon.

"We're more likely to find lodging in town," said Crimson.

"Crimson's right," said Phil. "We need to keep going, guys. We're almost there."

CHAPTER FOURTEEN

1875

The houses in 1875 were crumbling with decay. A number of buildings had suffered fires and had not been rebuilt. The place reeked of despair. As they moved through the streets, Del could feel eyes of suspicion and fear upon them. It reminded Del of their first day in Azdia when she and Phil had felt like they were being followed along the edge of the forest. Then it was only one creature, and it turned out to be Crimson. This time she felt as though they were trespassers in a town where there were likely thousands of eyes upon them and where something had gone terribly wrong.

"Should we say something?" Del asked.

"I'm not sure," answered Crimson. "This town is under the effects of the growing darkness. Perhaps we ought to just look around for your address."

"And hope it tells us something," said Phil.

As they passed through the streets there were houses that had no number, and there didn't appear to be any logical sequence to the numbers they did find. The first four numbers were almost always missing, giving just the address relative to their town. Crimson had explained that in his town every building had all eight numbers, even though the first four were always the same, because they took pride in Azdia. Here in 1875 no such pride seemed to exist.

"We're going to need to find someone to help us make sense of these streets, or I'm not sure how we'll find number 1889," said Crimson.

They shifted their search from finding the right building to finding someone who might be able to help them. Their search seemed in vain until they stumbled upon a lumen, sleeping and propped up against an old burnt out building. She was filthy. There was no visible glow to her at all, but perhaps it was covered by the rags that hung off her very bony body. Not one of them wished to approach her, but Crimson insisted they try.

He went over to her, and tried chirping a little, to no avail. He resorted to shaking her awake, and she came to with a start. She ignored Crimson and locked her gaze on Del. The lumen's eyes were wild. Del and the others stood their ground as the small dark figure limped toward them.

She stood in front of Del, grabbed her by the side of both of her arms and shouted, "Get out of here! You're not wanted. Nobody is wanted here!"

Del struggled to get free, but the grip on her was tight. Then Del saw her glow, but it wasn't like any other she had seen. It wasn't really a glow at all. It was black. And it passed through the lumen's body, heading from her chest out toward her hands. Phil and Guy were the closest to Del and tried to get the lumen off, but their blows seemed to simply bounce off her.

Crimson managed to latch onto her but was having a terrible time loosening her grip on Del.

Another lumen came flying out of a nearby building and pounced on the crazy one, peeling her fingers back and freeing Del from whatever was about to happen to her. The second lumen pinned the crazy one to the ground and chirped a few words as they struggled. The two ended in an embrace, with one stroking the hair of the other as they lay together in the middle of the road.

Del slumped to the ground, shivering. Her side seethed with pain. She'd been scared out of her skin, but it was the words that were left ringing in her ears - "You're not wanted." She didn't know why, but her thoughts drifted to home as her mind kept replaying those words.

Her eyes rolled into her head, and she could see her mother's face, but she had the eyes of the crazy lumen. She was saying over and over again, "You're not wanted; you're not wanted." Del longed for home, longed for a hug from her mother, but was at the same time terrified of returning to a family where love was absent. Del wished for a place where she was wanted, where she could learn to be herself and have no fear.

Behind her mother's voice, she could hear someone else, distant and muffled, but unmistakable. "Del - come back to us. We need you."

It was Sam. She followed that voice in her mind. Where was it? Her mother's demented eyes wouldn't seem to let her open her own. She could hear her Mother and sister's voices whispering to each other, saying things like: "Life is so much better without her around," and "We hope she never comes back."

She fought with her own thoughts of unworthiness

and rejection. She fought against the terrible pain in her side. Her whole body was shaking, and her mind was racing trying to get away from her mother and toward her best friend - to Sam.

She felt her lips move, and a weak voice exhaled "Sam... where are you?"

"I'm right here, Del." Sam sounded panicked now. "Del, you have to breathe. Del! Del!"

Del pictured herself running out of her house back on Farmer road. She tore down the street, and she could hear her mother's voice yelling after her, "That's right Del! Don't come back. You are not wanted!"

She just kept running as fast as she could toward Sam's house. It was hard to run because she could feel all her limbs shaking terribly, but she pressed on and tried to fight. In her dream, she felt like she was starting to black out. She could see Sam's front door at the centre of her tunnel vision. She burst through it, and behind the door was a blinding, beautiful light like no other she had ever seen. The light enveloped her and she felt it as much as she saw it. The light was the embrace she had been longing for from a parent, as though she had been dipped in love. Within an instant, it was gone.

She awoke from her breathless dream and sat bolt upright, eyes wide open. She breathed in a huge breath. "Sam?" she gasped.

"I'm here," Sam said holding her hand. "We thought you were... gone."

"We've had too many close calls with you," Phil chuckled, trying to make light of it in his own way. "You've really got to stop doing that."

Del took in the scene. The four of them lay on one

side of the street, the two strange lumens on the other, and Crimson was standing right in the middle, looking lost. Tears were again streaming down his cheeks. He walked over to Del and knelt in front of her.

"I didn't know it was this bad," Crimson said. "I didn't know the darkness had grown this much. I'm so sorry."

Del reached out and hugged him. "It's not your fault," she reassured him.

As she held him, Del felt different. She felt the light within him, and it was a version of the light from her dream.

"It's going to be okay," said Del.

She heard herself say the words, and for the first time in a long time, since even before they had been trapped in a strange and dangerous world, she believed them.

*****

The lumen that had tackled the crazy one was on her feet. "We can't stay on the street like this. We need to get indoors. Somewhere safe," she said.

She had touched Del when she peeled back the fingers of the crazy one. She must have learned the language then. Del wondered when they had become a "we".

Crimson wiped away his tears and looked at the crazy-eyed lumen that lay by herself breathing heavily, but now calm. "Can you keep her under control?"

"Yes. She's sick and needs some food and rest. But there's more like her who have gotten much worse, so we can't stay here. It's not safe. You need to trust me."

Del wasn't about to go anywhere with her attacker. Guy spoke up for her, "We can't go anywhere with that thing."

"I think we are out of options," Crimson said.

Phil made the final call. "What other choice do we have? I think we have to trust them, for now."

Del, Sam and Guy looked at each other with resignation as if to say that they didn't like it, but Phil was probably right.

Crimson spoke for the group. "Okay - we'll come with you."

The calm lumen helped the crazy one to her feet and called over her shoulder, "Follow me."

They scurried off down a nearby alley, with Crimson and the children following close behind. They ducked into a partially burnt building. The lumens led them down a flight of stairs. At the bottom, the calm one produced a key to unlock a heavy door that stood in their way. Behind the door, they found a well-equipped, though slightly dingy kitchen. There were stocks of food.

"This is where we've been hiding out... from the others," the calm one explained. "C'mon, let's get some food together for you."

Crimson lent a hand in the kitchen, introducing himself and the four children. He said nothing about them being the Malak. The calm lumen didn't ask any questions about the children's identity or what they were doing in Azdia. Rather, she simply introduced herself as Cinder and identified the crazy one as her sister, Pyria.

They stayed busy getting the food ready and laid it out on a large table. They sat around it with Cinder separating Pyria off from the rest of the group. Pyria began eating and drinking right away, as the children waited for the customary toast. Crimson raised his glass, as did Sam, Guy, Del and Phil. Cinder raised an eyebrow and smirked, but didn't touch her glass. She motioned to them to go ahead without her. With one accord, the group shouted out "To Mr. Thicket." Cinder couldn't contain herself any longer and burst out laughing.

"Mr. Thicket? Seriously?" she said through her chuckles. "You believe in Mr. Thicket?"

"Of course." Crimson replied.

"Okay, I guess. But…" Cinder turned to the children, "don't let him lead you astray, okay? There's no such person as Mr. Thicket. It's all just an old myth."

"What are you talking about?" said Crimson, annoyed.

"My grandmother used to tell me those stories when I was little, but we all knew that that's all they were - stories," said Cinder. "Just there to teach us to be nice to each other and to shine brightly, and to use any power you have moderately and for good. None of it is real."

"It's all real!" Crimson was flabbergasted. "I live not far from the Old Oak. I've been there many times. These two have been there too." He motioned toward Del and Phil.

"So what! Lots of people have seen the one tree that's different than the rest. It doesn't prove anything. Look, don't listen to him, no matter what he says. There is no such person as Mr. Thicket, and even if there was, just look around you. This Thicket is supposed to be the great protector and provider, but just look how much we're suffering now. They blame it on a growing darkness and are waiting for some beings nothing like us to show up and bring back the light or whatever. Nonsense!"

Then it dawned on Cinder. "Wait a minute," she said. "You think they're the Malak, don't you?"

Crimson looked down.

"You do!" Cinder continued. "Oh, that's a riot. This is the most priceless thing I've ever heard. They're just kids, and little Pyria here took one of them down in a matter of seconds!"

Crimson looked lost for words as Cinder kept going. "Look, the lumens around here are getting sick. It's not a growing darkness; it's a disease or something. We haven't quite figured it out, but... we will. They're not turning to the dark side or something crazy like that. Now, if there was some Thicket fellow out there somewhere who cared about us, and loved us, and supposedly protected us, why would he let all of us get sick? And look how it's happening - those who are sick attack the healthy - it's not right... And don't you start talking about the dark times and the hope for the Malak. That's all just a story to keep us in line."

Sam, of all people, piped up. "I thought you said it was a story to teach you how to be nice and good."

"Well..." Cinder stumbled in her words. "Yes, that too. Both things really. The stories are there to teach us things, but they've been used to keep us in line, and in the eighteenth province, we don't go for that sort of thing anymore. Look, I'm not trying to be mean - I'm just trying to tell you the truth. This is just the way it is. It is up to us to figure out a cure to help ourselves get better. Any talk of Thicket and Malak is useless."

"I can see talking to you about it is useless," Crimson

said.

"Look, I'm sorry. Okay. Let's just eat, and we can talk about something else," said Cinder.

"Can we talk about how we're going to get home?" Guy asked.

*****

Phil took over the table conversation. "We need to find a certain address. We need to find 1889."

"Why would you need to go there?" Cinder asked.

"All we know is that we need to go beyond it and then 'through the place of the tallest lumber,'" Sam explained, quoting the riddle.

"Well, it's easy enough to get you there, assuming we can dodge any of the sick lumens, but I don't think you want to be going into the Violet Wood."

"You know where we need to go?" said Phil.

"Well, 1889 would be right around the edge of the Violet Wood, and there's no other forest anywhere near here that has taller trees than that place - they're enormous. That would be the place of the tallest lumber."

"Can you take us there?" Phil asked.

"I could take you to the edge, but I'm not going in. No way! And you shouldn't go in either."

"Why won't you go in?" Del asked.

"There are feldroes in there. Big ones and ferocious," said Cinder. "They'll bite your head off or swallow you whole if they get half a chance."

"Feldroes will?" asked Phil.

"Feldroes wouldn't ever do that," said Crimson.

"The feldroes in the Violet Wood will," said Cinder.

"Don't get sucked in, any of you. You'd all be better off to go back from where you came."

"But that's the problem," said Phil. "We need to follow a riddle given to us in order to get back to our home."

"A riddle, eh? What's the rest of the riddle, then?" Cinder's eyes widened.

Before anyone could stop him, Sam blurted out the whole thing.

Carry yourselves beyond the number
Through the place of the tallest lumber.
Seek the one from whom under you slid,
Whose name you found when only you hid.
Within this one's fence, the door shall appear.
You won't see if you look, but you will if you hear.

"Well, well," said Cinder. "It seems you're looking for someone who lives on the other side of the Violet Wood. I wonder if he's still living there."

"Who?" cried the children in unison.

"There is someone who used to live out on the opposite edge of the Violet Wood. He had a bit of a funny name."

Del thought this was rich, considering the names they had already encountered in Azdia.

Cinder continued. "Old Blythe they called him. Always kept to himself, though, never had much to do with anyone or anything. I can't see that he'd be able to help you with anything. Always heard he was a bit strange, y'know."

"Is he a lumen?" Crimson asked.

"Of course he's a lumen! There are stories that he's not, that he's some kind of magician or something, but like I said before, they're just stories."

Del was about to burst. "You guys. The name. The name on the stone. The gravestone? Remember what it was? Blythe. This is for sure who we are looking for. It all fits."

"We're going then," Phil announced. "Cinder, you've got to show us the way. We've got to leave as soon as we can."

Sam whispered to Del. "It doesn't totally fit. One line of the riddle doesn't work. 'Seek the one from whom under you slid.' We weren't under the gravestone. We were on top of it."

"It doesn't matter, Sam. It's close enough," said Del.

"I don't know," said Sam. "I think we might be looking for two people or something."

"I guess we'll see when we get there," said Del.

"I guess so," said Sam.

CHAPTER FIFTEEN

The Violet Wood

Cinder led them quietly through the streets of 1875, sticking to the narrowest alleys to avoid meeting anyone on a main road. They had left Pyria behind. Cinder's rationale was that they had a long walk and Pyria was not well. Crimson argued that Pyria was a liability to staying quiet and unnoticed. Del just felt safer without her attacker around.

It wasn't long before Cinder stopped the group in front of a house. There was nothing spectacular about it. It was burnt out and looked abandoned, but the address could be seen clearly. Surprisingly for this city, it had all eight numbers: 1875 - 1889. Seeing it, Del was taken back to the day that seemed months away now, when she had first discovered the gravestone with those numbers on it. She pictured it and the name that accompanied it. Blythe was a bit of a strange name; Cinder was right about that.

The only distinguishing feature of the place was that it was set back a bit from the other houses, creating a break in the row of buildings. This allowed them to see what was behind the buildings for the first time. Towering above the lumen-made structures were trees. Their trunks were as wide as cars, and their tops looked as though they were touching the thick grey clouds. The leaves of the trees were changing. There were greens, mixed with yellows and oranges. Other than their size, the trees were spectacular in another respect. Their bark was a deep shade of purple: the Violet Wood.

"This is as far as I go," Cinder said. "I still think you're all crazy for going in there. Good luck."

Cinder turned and headed back down the alley mumbling to herself. "Never see them again" was all Del could catch before Cinder was out of earshot and presumably on her way back home.

Phil, Del, Guy, and Sam, led once again by Crimson, slipped through a very small gap between the houses in front of them to get to the forest behind. There wasn't much of a backyard to this place. The first tree was almost right on top of the house. This forest was quite different than anything else they had seen in Azdia. It was not just that it had immense purple trees, but that the forest seemed open and airy. It was much less dense, with the trees well-spaced out from each other, and very little undergrowth. Even with the size, the forest seemed much less menacing than the one that had repeatedly attacked them.

There was something else that was strange about these trees. The bark was glossy. Up close, the trees looked as though they were made of glass. Del wasn't sure why, but they reminded her of the glass stone from the graveyard. She touched one, and it felt like glass as well. They looked as though someone had built hundreds of thousands of giant purple glass sculptures and then stuck a whole bunch of leaves on them.

Crimson walked up to a tree and laid his hand on it. Within seconds, he had let go without any conversation.

"I can see why Cinder was so afraid," he said. "Total silence."

"The trees aren't talking?" Del asked.

"No. They're dead. All of them. The forest is dead."

*****

"Good," said Guy. "Can't attack us then."

"It's generally not the trees we should worry about," said Crimson. "If this forest is home to feldroes like Cinder said, they won't be happy about their forest dying off. Feldroes won't make the best of it. They will blame someone, even if it's irrational. Most likely, they will blame us because we're here."

"We have no choice, though," said Phil. "We've got to go in."

They entered the forest and immediately saw why there was so little undergrowth. It had been trampled, over and over again, by the giant beasts that made this place their home. It made for easy walking for Crimson and the children.

The forest continued to feel nice and open, and the changing colors on the trees, although they knew it was because of death, looked beautiful in the sunlight that was breaking through the clouds above. The canopy of the forest was so high that it could very well have been the sky. Filtered light shone through the leaves of orange and red onto the glossy purple trunks to make a delicate display. Del had never seen anything so enchanting.

"Sam, what do you think we will need to do when we find the house of Old Blythe?" Phil asked as they walked.

"The riddle seems to say that a door will appear in his backyard," Sam offered. "That's the part that says 'within this one's fence.' I'm thinking maybe it'll be like it was under the hedge back in the church yard. We'll find something like the glass, and it'll open up a way to get back home. The weird thing is that the riddle says 'You won't see if you look, but you will if you hear.'"

"What does that mean?" Phil asked.

"I'd guess that it means we aren't supposed to look for whatever will open the door," said Sam. "We're supposed to hear something. We're supposed to listen."

"So, we find the house, get inside the fence, stand there and listen?" Guy asked.

"And then hope something happens," concluded Sam.

"I guess when we get there we'll know if this was all a big waste of time," said Phil.

Del had been thinking about her family again and decided to bring it up with all of them. "Are none of you worried about our families? We've been gone for so long."

"Of course we are, Del," Phil reassured. "But, what can we do? We have to just keep trying to get home."

Time passed. Del forgot that they were in any danger. She almost forgot that they were in a forest. It was like walking in a never-ending palace filled with pillars of royal purple. It was serene. But then, she heard a noise.

Phil held up his hand, indicating that the company should stop. "Shhh. Listen."

They stood in silence.

"It sounds like another waterfall," Guy suggested.

"It could be," Phil agreed. "It is definitely up ahead. We should still keep moving, I think."

The sound quickly got louder.

"That's not water," Crimson said. "It's a stampede! We've got to turn back. Now!"

Before they could figure out what was happening, the great creatures appeared on the horizon before them. Who knows how many feldroes were racing toward them. The children and Crimson turned and fled, but the beasts were already upon them. The first ones simply passed them by as the children did what they could to avoid their great legs.

"I don't think they're after us, but we can't outrun them!" Crimson shouted. "We need to find cover."

"There's nothing here!" Phil cried.

"The trees." Sam shouted.

The sound from the feldroes was deafening and the ground shook beneath them.

"They won't be touching the trees," Sam yelled. "Look at the ground. There've been stampedes before, and not a single tree is down. Get as close as you can to a tree on the back side of it."

They followed Sam's advice. Crimson, Del, and Sam clung to the back of the tree closest to them. Phil and Guy were together on another tree. The feldroes raced by. Even though she had ridden on one before, Del never could have imagined they were capable of this kind of pace. Even Crimson looked surprised at what he was seeing. Nothing contained his look of shock and terror at what came next, however. The last feldroe from the herd passed them by and as they watched it go, they discovered the reason for the stampede.

Diving from high above was a black winged creature. It was more bat-like than bird-like, with a kind of skin stretched out to make its wings. Del didn't get a good look at its face, but she could clearly see claws protruding from under its outstretched wings. It was massive, and as it dove, it picked up incredible speed. It caught up to the last of the feldroes, with talons extended. It struck. The winged creature took down the feldroe with remarkable ease. The feldroe crumpled under the attack and crashed to the forest floor. The children and Crimson were close enough to feel the great thud as the massive beast hit the ground.

Phil and Guy looked over at Crimson who, with a terrified look, indicated for them all to get lower to the ground and get on the other side of the trees they were clinging to. Part of Del wished Crimson could extend his power to make them all tiny again to hide from the foul creature they had just observed, but she knew he couldn't. He wouldn't have the strength to bring them back.

As some of the dust settled and the sound of the stampede dissipated, Crimson and the children peaked out from behind the trees to see where the thing had gone. Hopefully, it had kept up its chase of the herd. But there was no such luck. The winged creature was perched on top of the dead feldroe. It was a hunter and a carnivore. It wanted the feldroe's meat, and it was getting its fill. Del couldn't watch the terrible sight before her.

Crimson signalled that they should try to sneak away. Without saying a word, they all backed away from their trees. They began by crawling; then once they had gotten far enough, they risked walking. Still, no one said a word until some time later, when overhead they saw a whoosh of black. It was the creature, carrying a large portion of feldroe meat. Then it was gone.

Del broke the silence. "Crimson, what was that?"

"I don't know," Crimson replied. "That creature was like nothing I've ever seen. Perhaps the ancient darkness has fully returned and is showing its might. The land will change, whole species will be killed off, and it might be beginning right here in this forest."

Crimson and the children kept moving. The Violet Wood was beautiful, but, as Cinder had warned them, incredibly dangerous. The faster they could cross it, the better. They ate some of their provisions without stopping. It was as though they had an unspoken agreement that they would not stop until they found Old Blythe's house or until they simply could not go any further for exhaustion.

*****

As they walked in silence, a cry rang out high above. They were not alone.

"It's come back," Phil said.

"And it's brought friends," said Guy.

Three black winged creatures circled above them.

"We must find some cover somewhere," Crimson said.

But none could be found. One of the creatures began a dive towards them.

"Run, children! Run!" Crimson shouted.

Crimson stood his ground as the children took off.

"Stay close to the trunks of the trees," said Sam. "It will be harder for them to grab you if you're right next

159

to a tree trunk." They followed his instructions, darting from one tree to the next.

As the four friends quickly retreated, Del looked back and saw Crimson bravely facing off against the evil creature. Crimson didn't stand a chance. The creature picked up speed in its dive and headed straight for the defenceless lumen. Crimson did not flinch for a moment, until the very last second, until the very last inch of space. Just as the creature was about to strike what was sure to be a killer blow, Crimson dodged to one side, reached out, and touched the belly of the beast. One of the mighty talons stretched out and grabbed Crimson around the waist. He didn't seem hurt, but the creature had him. They ascended together high up near the canopy of color above them. From below, it looked like the creature was holding a flashlight in its claw. Crimson was glowing.

Del took all this in in an instant, then stopped the boys with a yell. "Guys, look at that."

They all stopped running and gazed at the amazing sight above them, backdropped by the dancing of orange, yellow and red lit leaves. Crimson had changed himself into one of the winged creatures. Crimson's version was grey with a red glow coming from within. The children now had a view of their lizard-like faces, ferocious and angry. Crimson's looked good, however, and a little mischievous. He seemed to revel in the idea that he had turned the tables on his attacker.

If Crimson had been facing off against just one of them, he might have had a chance. The real problem was that he was outnumbered. The three creatures attacked together, and Crimson fought valiantly. They grabbed at one another, bit and scratched. They exchanged powerful blows. Crimson glared in the direction of the children as if to say, "What are you still doing here?"

"He's not going to win," Del cried.

"He's not trying to win," Phil declared. "He's trying to give us a chance to escape - and we're blowing it. We've got to go."

The words had barely left Phil's lips when one of the creatures connected with a blow to Crimson's head with its tail, sending him spiralling to the ground. The three creatures dove in pursuit. Crimson's body landed with a thud. His whole body became consumed with his own interior light. Brighter and brighter he shone as though he might explode. The creatures backed off their attack, and Crimson's body went into convulsions as it transformed into his regular form. The bright light dissipated and all they could see was the small bruised body of their lumen friend. His inner light flickered briefly; then it quickly dimmed to nothing. One of the creatures picked him up in its talon and flew up and away.

Crimson was gone.

CHAPTER SIXTEEN

Rescued by the Rider

Tears streamed down Del's cheeks at the terrible thought of Crimson's death and the terrible feeling of being alone.

Phil pulled her away. "We have to go," he whispered. "We've stayed too long already. We're next for those things."

The two remaining creatures turned their attention to the four children, who took off as fast as they could. The children's legs were no match whatsoever for the winged power of the beasts. Within four or five flaps, they were ready for their dive against the children.

Guy streaked ahead, with Phil next, followed by Del and Sam who ran side by side. The first dive came toward Del and Sam. Del could feel the pace of the thing without even turning to look. At the last second, she yelled, "Drop!" She and Sam dove to the ground and a rush of wind flew by them. The claw-talons outstretched above them nearly caught them. Had they been a split second slower, Sam would have been struck down right there. Del had thought the attacks of the forest had been bad, but it was painfully clear to her now that any blow they would have suffered there would have done minor harm to them. The speed and power of these things were such that if they made a proper connection to one of their legs or arms, they might just tear it straight off.

"The next one won't make that same mistake," Del said. "We can't run in the open like this."

"We're done for, no matter what," said Sam. "We can't beat those things. We're just kids."

"C'mon." Del led Sam to the nearest tree and looked to see where they could go next. The creature that had missed them circled back and barrelled toward them at high speed with no regard for the massive tree that Del and Sam stood beside. Del and Sam dove out of the way again and the creature's talons collided with the trunk. It shattered and purple glass flew everywhere. The blow to the tree wasn't enough to knock it down, but shards of glass rained down on the two children.

Sam and Del got to their feet and stared aghast as the second creature descended upon Phil. It was like watching something in slow motion. The thing dropped from above, closer and closer. Phil tried the same tactic as Del and Sam: he dropped to the ground at the last second. The creature, though, did not fly by. It reacted by flapping its great wings twice, hovering for a moment and landing right next to their friend. Phil flipped over to face his attacker. The beast stood high above Phil, craned its neck, and let out a bellowing howl-like roar as if proclaiming victory.

"We've got to do something," Del said as she ran a few steps toward Phil and the creature.

"Hey you!" she yelled. "Pick on someone your own

size!"

She didn't know what else to say. She was trying to sound tough, but she knew it didn't matter what she said. All she was doing was maybe buying Phil and the rest of them a few more seconds of breathing. Soon, their lives would be over. Del, though, would not give up without a fight. The creature turned toward her and looked disinterested. It looked back down at Phil and prepared to strike.

Sam jumped to Del's side, wearing a look that she had never seen before. He held a rock in his hand.

"Too scared to come after two of us?" Sam said. "Come on, you piece of filth. I will tear you to shreds with my bare hands right now."

Del realized how pathetic her attempt had been. Was this really Sam next to her? Not for long, it wasn't. He left her side, running at pace toward the creature, hurling insults as he went. The creature turned its head toward Sam just in time to be met in the face with the rock hurled from Sam's hands. The beast roared angrily, and once Sam was close enough, it swatted him easily aside with its tail.

Del couldn't believe Sam's bravery, as ill-conceived as it was. He lay motionless near a tree, but it looked like he was okay. Phil had managed to get to his feet and start running, but he was easily cut off by the creature who simply leaped, flapped its wings once, and dropped directly in front of him. This was clearly the end. Just beyond Phil, Del could see Guy standing off against the other creature. There was absolutely nothing she could do. She had watched these things kill Crimson, and now she would see her best friends suffer the same fate; then she would be next.

*****

Del nearly passed out from the fear that gripped her. Her vision became fuzzy around the edges, and everything began fading to black. She'd never quite known what it meant to have a swimmy head, but now she did. It felt just as if her brain was underwater, and she couldn't catch her breath. It took her back instantly to being submerged and sinking in the black lake, just before the transformed Crimson had saved her. But Crimson would not be coming to their rescue this time.

She was pulled from her mentally submerged state by a piercing screech. The sound, like nails on a chalkboard times ten, came from above and behind her. Adrenaline pumped through her body, causing her tunnel vision to disappear. Instinctively, she whipped around and looked up to see a large raven-like bird with cream colored feathers, soaring toward the creature that was bearing down on Phil. The sound was not coming from the bird, however, but from its rider. A man sat atop the bird. Not a lumen, but a real man. He had the look of a warrior, strong and muscular. He had long sun-soaked hair and tanned leathery skin. He held a long dagger in one hand and reins that were attached into the raven's beak, in the other.

The man opened his mouth and bellowed out the high pitched screech a second time. This time, the two black creatures seemed to writhe in pain when they heard it. In the middle of his yell, as the raven flew past, the man leaped from the back of his feathered steed onto the creature beside Phil. The man's dagger went up, and in one quick motion, he had stabbed the creature in the back of its long neck. The second creature flew off quickly with the cream colored raven in pursuit. The wounded creature staggered a few steps and flapped its wings in a failed attempt to fly. It keeled over and lay on the forest floor defeated. The man walked over to it, removed his dagger and placed it in a sheath hidden beneath a grey cloak.

The children, motionless, stared at the stranger. Del didn't know what to do. Fortunately, he didn't give them much time to consider their next course of action.

"Come," he said. "You're not safe in this wood. I can get you out, but we must go now."

With that, he turned from the children and began walking away at a quick pace. He did not look back to see if they were following him.

The four friends ran to each other.

"What should we do?" Guy asked.

"He's probably our best shot to getting out of here," said Phil. "And he did rescue us. Sam, what do you think?"

Sam looked a little surprised at this rare consultation, but Del supposed that this was because Sam seemed to have the best handle on the riddle.

Sam pondered for a second or two, then said, "Old Blythe's place is supposed to be that way, but he's heading that way." Sam pointed in two very different directions. "I still feel like we should be heading to Old Blythe's, but I agree we should probably follow him. He saved us, and we have no idea how long it'll take to find Old Blythe's place. Besides, there's something about the riddle that makes me think we are supposed to find someone else before we go to Old Blythe's. Maybe this guy can help us with that."

"It's settled," said Phil. "Let's go."
The children ran to catch up to their rescuer.

*****

After having caught up to the man, Phil, jogging to keep up with his gait, tried asking him a few questions. Things like: What's your name? Where did you come from? How did you know we were in trouble? What were those black things with the wings? Each time he asked anything, he got a kind of grunt in return.

Finally the man spoke up. "There'll be plenty of time for questions when we get out of this wood. Won't be long now. We must press on." And that was that. No more talking to the stranger-rescuer.

He led the children through the Violet Wood without any further difficulty or altercation. The forest itself, however, was becoming much more dense. Was he leading them out of the forest or further into the heart of it? Trees were closer together and instead of clearings or wide feldroe-trampled paths, there was actual underbrush. Not a lot of it, but enough that their route was blocked several times, and they needed to find ways around.

The man stopped in front of an area covered in ferns and other short, rather healthy looking plants. Around them were several saplings that looked alive and well.

"This forest is dead, so I've been planting new trees in the hopes that there will still be something here," the man said.

He cleared away some of the plants, and there, flat along the ground, was a door. It wasn't anything impressive, not an energy portal capable of transporting them home, just a plain wooden door with no engravings or any other noticeable features other than a gold knob, a gold knocker and a keyhole. The man reached into his shirt and from a chain around his neck he produced a gold key. Bending down, the man used it to unlock the door. He turned the handle and pulled it open. A flight of stairs descended into the ground.

"This is your best chance to survive," said the man. "You don't want to spend a night in this wood, believe me."

Del was apprehensive. Following a stranger was one thing, and they were getting used to taking those kinds of risks; following a stranger into a closed basement-like room was something else altogether.

"I'm not sure about this," Phil said bravely.

The man replied, "It is your choice entirely, of course. I can point you in the best and perhaps safest direction, but trust me, you'd be a whole lot safer in here with me than out there with them."

"Can we wait out here for a while and think about it?"

"Absolutely. But you could all do with some food, couldn't you? I'll go get some and bring it out if you're determined not to come in." The man disappeared down the staircase.

"I'm not going down there," said Sam.

"That's just 'cause you're afraid of the dark," said Guy.

"I went in the church basement," said Sam.

"That was a church, though," said Guy.

"Ya - and this is a strange stairway in the middle of nowhere leading to who knows where and who knows what! This is the nightmare scenario," said Sam. "If our parents ever warned us about something, it is this thing right here. Never follow a stranger. Never get in a car with a stranger. Never go into a stranger's house. Let's face it - this is totally what you'd see on the news. Man traps four children in his bomb shelter and does horrible things to them. We've gotta get away from here."

"Sam, calm down," said Phil. "You're going off the deep end. Remember where we are. We're in Azdia. We don't have the option of just calling our parents. In fact, we're out of options. I say we see what food he brings up, we'll eat, then we'll decide what to do."

The man returned. He took the time and effort to spread a green and red checkered picnic blanket out on the ground for them. This was a nice touch but couldn't make up for the small portions nor the bland taste of what the man had to offer. Guy made a face when he tried a piece of dried fruit.

Del said to him under her breath, "He's trying his best."

"How do you know he's not trying to poison us?" Guy whispered back.

"I think if he was trying to kill us, he would have just let those things back there finish the job," Del said.

While the children sat on the blanket eating, the man paced back and forth, keeping his gaze far away.

Phil was deep in thought. Then he spoke, "We're going down the stairs. We have no other option. It'll be suicide to stay out here in the forest. This guy is a little weird, but he did save us. And... we have each other."

Sam swallowed slowly. "This might be a bigger mistake than going through the portal in the graveyard."

"I agree with you," said Phil. "But can any of you think of any better option?"

Del, Guy, and Sam looked blankly back at Phil. No one had any other ideas, but none of them were feeling right about walking down an unknown staircase with a stranger either.

They were starting to lose light, and the man was becoming increasingly agitated, darting his gaze in a wide circle around their picnic spot.

"Are you done, yet?" he asked the children. "Have you decided?"

"We're coming with you," Phil said. Then he added, "but first you have to tell us your name."

The man re-opened the door on the ground, bowed low, and said, "Mr. Thicket, at your service."

CHAPTER SEVENTEEN

Mr. Thicket

The children sat in shock on the blanket as their rescuer disappeared down the staircase. He was Mr. Thicket? Mr. Thicket, the keeper and protector of Azdia, had rescued them? Del's mind raced, trying to imagine what might be at the bottom of Mr. Thicket's stairs. Was this where he lived? Did he have a plan? Would he also think they were the Malak?

"But he's so… young," Sam said.

"And blonde," Guy said. They all laughed.

"He's not at all what I pictured either," said Del.

"If the stories are true, at least we'll all be safe," said Phil.

Mr. Thicket's head appeared out of the ground. "I thought you said you were coming?"

His head disappeared, then reappeared just as quick. There was a mischievous twinkle in his eye, as though he knew that he had just blown their minds with the revelation of his identity.

"And bring my blanket," he continued. "And close the door behind you."

His head disappeared again. The children got up, and Sam collected the blanket. They filed down the staircase. Del, last down, closed the door.

They could see a glow of firelight below them as they descended the steep staircase. They didn't get very far, maybe twenty or twenty five steps, when the tunnel turned into a large open cavern. The stairs continued down, bounded on one side by a wall lined with torches, and on the other side a steep drop-off. The cavern was deep, and the bottom of it imperceptible.

The children, petrified of falling off the one side of the staircase, clung to the torch-wall. Mr. Thicket, however, almost danced down the stairs, seemingly paying no attention to the drop of doom just inches from his feet. Every now and again, he turned around completely and walked down the stairs backwards to speak to the children.

"C'mon children," he said several times. "So glad you decided to come." Or, "Good decision, good decision," or a few times he said, "Just wait until you see what's at the bottom."

The children tried their best to keep up without plummeting to their deaths. Down they went into the depths, not knowing whether to be excited or terrified. Del hoped that somehow this trip down the stairs would turn things around for them. Maybe, somehow, these stairs would lead them home.

*****

A din rose up from below them. They could hear what sounded like birds, not the chirping or singing of songbirds, but much more like the incessant squawks of crows or ravens. Along with the bird sounds, there were lumen chirps. Although a cacophony, it did sound joyful, as though there was a party or festival taking place. There was laughter, and even some singing. Yes, that is exactly what they could hear as they got closer. There were lumens singing what sounded like a very happy song. The birds tried to join in, but their heavy squawks overpowered the melody. When this happened, several lumens broke out in their own version of laughter. Then the song continued.

Hearing the merriment lifted Del's spirit. If there were happy lumens down there, they must have made the right choice in trusting Mr. Thicket.

When they got to the bottom of the cavern, they heard the lumens shushing one another. All went silent. Carved into two of the cavern walls were all different three dimensional scenes: pictures of lumens, human beings, birds, feldroes, boats, and all kinds of other things. Perhaps these told some history of Azdia or held some other significance. Along one wall were a series of life-sized statues of various human beings and lumens.

Along the last wall were twelve perches upon which sat eleven birds. The birds were just like the one they had seen Mr. Thicket riding during the rescue, but each was a different color. The open perch was clearly for Mr. Thicket's cream-colored bird which had flown in pursuit of the winged creature but had not yet returned.

At the centre of the room was a banquet table with mountains of delicious looking food. It was set with five places, presumably for Mr. Thicket and the four children. The table cloth looked as though it was made of actual silver, and each place had a gold plate, gold cutlery and a gold goblet. The chairs looked like royal thrones, with the one at the head looking the largest and most elaborate. Everything was perfect. The only thing that seemed out of place were five plain looking stools that sat next to each chair. The stools were higher than the table top and each one had a small ladder attached to it.

There was no more singing or laughter. It had been replaced by beautiful music, played by a quartet of lumens huddled in one corner of the room playing some strange looking instruments. The children and Mr. Thicket were greeted by a line of smiling lumens. The first in the line bowed low. Mr. Thicket extended his hand, the lumen grasped it and looked up expectantly. Mr. Thicket smiled back. The lumen and Mr. Thicket walked along the line as though this was a military inspection. A lumen came over to the children and directed them to follow Mr. Thicket, single file. Phil went first. The next lumen in line bowed low to Phil as the first one had to Mr. Thicket. He also extended his hand to Phil. Phil hesitated and looked over his shoulder at his friends. They shrugged at him. Phil took the lumen's hand, who returned from the bow and escorted Phil along the waiting line of lumens. This was repeated for Guy, Sam, and last of all, Del.

The lumens led them to their prepared places at the table. The children and Mr. Thicket stood in front of their chairs waiting. The children didn't know what they were waiting for, but Mr. Thicket wasn't sitting down, so they didn't sit down either.

Del imagined that this was what dining at some fancy state dinner at the White House or with the Queen of England would be like. Except here, their servants were lumens, they were in a subterranean hide-out, and one of the feature decorations were birds that were larger than a person. It certainly was a strange state dinner. For the first time, Del noticed that the lumens were not glowing. Perhaps their glow was hidden by their clothes which looked like formal uniforms going all the way up to their neck, but it didn't seem like it. In all her time in Azdia, she had yet to see lumens look this happy, however.

The music came to a halt. Mr. Thicket cleared his throat. "Well done, all of you!" he said. He clapped his hands twice and sat down. There was a flurry of activity. The lumens that had escorted them in raced up the ladders and perched atop the stools next to each place setting. The musicians resumed their playing. All the other lumens scurried off out of the room. The children stood, speechless.

"Come, my friends. Sit and feast. You are safe and sound now, here with us." Mr. Thicket beamed.

The children sat, not quite knowing what else to do. They watched Mr. Thicket. He pointed to food on the table that he wanted and said "I'll have a bit of this" or "a bit of that" or "lots of that" and his perched lumen would reach from the stool, or jump from it and deliver Mr. Thicket's food to his plate. He looked up, as the children were not doing anything.

"Go on," Mr. Thicket said. "That's what they're there for."

Instead of requesting food, Del grabbed the goblet in her hands. She noticed it was already filled with some kind of drink. Phil, Guy, and Sam quickly followed Del's lead. They had said the toast before every meal on board Hollow's boat, the Zephyr, but it never felt fully real. This time, Mr. Thicket had rescued them first hand. He had protected them and provided for them directly. He had shown them true hospitality.

The four of them together, joyfully, loudly, toasted their host with all their vocal might. "To Mr. Thicket!"

The music stopped instantly. The lumens smiles dropped to looks of shock. Nobody in the room moved. What just happened? A look of anger flashed across Mr. Thicket's face, but it quickly went back to his smile. Then he let out a little chuckle.

"We never say that down here," Mr. Thicket said. "I know it is said out there, but I've never liked it too much. All that attention isn't necessary. I am who I am, and I do what I can. You didn't know to not make a fuss of me. So, no harm done. Let's have the music again."

Mr. Thicket clapped his hands twice, and the musicians started up again. The children slowly lowered their goblets. That was strange, Del thought. The boys seemed to take it in stride and just started doing what Mr. Thicket was doing, pointing at their food to order up what they wanted.

Del did the same. She pointed, and her lumen servant happily jumped to work. The food was unbelievably good, better than the best banquet they had had on the Zephyr.

*****

They ate for a few minutes without saying anything.

Then Del looked Mr. Thicket in the eyes, and said, "Why isn't there any light in them?"

"Oh, you are a brave one, asking a question that gets right to the heart of the matter," Mr. Thicket replied. "I like that."

Del just held her gaze.

Mr. Thicket continued: "I could tell you that they do in fact have a light glowing that is hidden by their clothes. Or I could tell you that they are a particular kind of lumen that has no light. But you deserve the truth. You are right - these lumens do not have light. What you do not know is what most lumens do not know... or do not want to believe. Their light is what kills them. As lumens get older and near death, their lights do not not grow dimmer, but get brighter. Shapeshifting is always painful, they tell me, but it is always over quickly. At the end of their lives, however, lumens spontaneously change into all the forms that they have ever taken. They can't control it, and it's terribly painful. It is a truly terrible thing to see, but an even worse thing to experience."

Del thought about what it felt like when Crimson had changed their sizes. The feeling afterward had been fantastic, but the actual change could very well be described as painful and confusing.

Mr. Thicket continued talking: "When lumens die, they become pure light. They believe that, as their rescuer, I somehow collect their light and hold it in safety forever. The problem is, they are wrong. Nothing happens to their light. It just disappears. Their life is over, and that's it. One thing they have right is that I am their rescuer; they just don't know the way I will ultimately save them all. You see, I've found a way to remove their light without them dying. Without them dying, ever. The lumens you see here will live forever."

"But can these lumens change shape?" Del asked.

"No. Nor can they talk to living things through their touch. But this is a small price to pay for everlasting life and the freedom from pain. And these lumens are already learning our language, as you've seen. They already have a basic understanding."

"We haven't heard any of them speak though," said Del.

"They aren't very comfortable with their speaking voices in other languages yet. Once they gain a little more confidence, they will be able to communicate. They do, after all, have all the time in the world to learn."

"So, the lumens losing their light back in 1875, that's because of you?" Phil asked.

"I know it looks bad there," said Mr. Thicket. "When lumens begin losing their light, they are labelled as 'sick' by others. They are ostracized and isolated. Usually the dark lumens run away once the change is complete for fear of being rejected by their friends and family. I provide them safety here. Eventually though, all lumens will be dark, and none of them will need to worry."

"This all seems very backward from what we would ever have thought," Guy chimed in. "Shouldn't light be good and darkness be bad?"

"That is the prevailing belief," Mr. Thicket answered. "And that belief is in fact my greatest enemy. If we could overcome that belief in Azdia, we could rescue all the lumens in one swoop."

"Why don't you just tell the lumens what you are telling us?" asked Sam. "You're Mr. Thicket after all."

"You four have been in Azdia only a little while. The lumens have lived here forever. If I was to just tell them this, most of them would reject it even though I am Mr. Thicket. The change from light to dark will mean a total change in how they live and in so much of what they believe. It must be done gradually, for their sakes. Eventually, enough of them will see that this is the way to everlasting life, and they will welcome the changes. But for now, it must be this way."

"So why are you telling us all this?" Phil asked.

"Like I said, I think you deserve the truth," said Mr. Thicket. "But tell me, what were the four of you doing in the Violet Wood? You are surely a long way from home."

"We're not from here, from Azdia, I mean," said Phil. "We're trying to find our way home, and we've been following clues to find something that can help us."

"Do you know what you are looking for?" Mr. Thicket asked.

"Not exactly. But the clues led us to the Violet Wood. We had a guide helping us, but when we were attacked by those black things, he was..." Phil's voice trailed off.

"I understand," said Mr. Thicket. "Perhaps I can provide some guidance and help you get home. Do you know where your guide was leading you?"

"We think we are supposed to head to a place called Old Blythe's cottage," said Phil. "Do you know where that is?"

"Of course I do," said Mr. Thicket. "I have kept an eye on Old Blythe for many years, and I can most certainly take you there. But you should know that Old Blythe can be very dangerous. He comes across as an absent-minded old man, but he is cunning and deceitful. It will be very important to not be taken in by him. You said you don't know what you are looking for, but it makes sense that Old Blythe might have something that could help you. He collects things, you see, and he would be particularly proud of possessing any magical object. Was it magic that brought you here?"

"I would say so," said Guy. "But everything seems pretty magical here!"

"I suppose the unfamiliar would seem magical," said Mr. Thicket, "Old Blythe would likely want to hide or protect the object you might be looking for. But I can most definitely help you."

They had finished eating, and lumens were scurrying, clearing and cleaning the tables.

"We should say good night," said Mr. Thicket. "Your lumens will show you to your rooms for the night when you're ready for some rest. We'll discuss our plans tomorrow and hopefully have you on your way home."

He motioned to the lumens who stood ready to take the children to their rooms.

CHAPTER EIGHTEEN

The Plan to Get Home

The children were finally alone, just the four of them. Their lumens had escorted them from the great hall down a beautifully decorated tunnel that had a series of wooden doors. Each of them had their own rooms and found, for the first time in Azdia, that they had very spacious accommodations. Each room contained a double bed, a dresser, and an easy chair. It was like being in a fancy hotel. The stone floor had been carved to look like tile, and, leading to the bed, there was a beautiful, soft rug. Each of the children had tried out the beds right away and found the comfort level to be top notch. After exploring each other's rooms, they met together in Phil's room.

"I can't believe you don't like him, Del," said Guy, "He is so awesome! I always thought this 'To Mr. Thicket' stuff was lame, but now I get it. He's cool."

"But he's changing the lumens from who they really are," said Del.

"He's saving them, changing them so that they never have pain and never die," said Phil. "That has to be good."

"Sam what do you think?" Del asked. Sam sat silently, unresponsive. "Sam," she repeated. "Sam!"

"What? What is it?" said Sam, as if waking up from a dream.

"What do you think?" Del said. "Can Mr. Thicket be trusted?"

"I don't know," Sam said. "But, there's something about the riddle that's bugging me."

"Oh, the riddle again," said Guy. "Can't you see that the old priest gave us that riddle to get us all killed? He sent us into that forest and then every step of the way things have tried to stop us or hurt us!"

"Shut up, Guy!" said Del. "What is it, Sam? Tell us."

Sam looked down at the ground.

"Well, spit it out, Sam," said Guy.

"It's okay, Sam," said Phil, with an encouraging tone. "We need to hear all the ideas."

Sam began. "So we haven't really gotten very far on the riddle. Think about it." He recited it again to remind his friends.

Carry yourselves beyond the number
Through the place of the tallest lumber.
Seek the one from whom under you slid,
Whose name you found when only you hid.
Within this one's fence, the door shall appear.
You won't see if you look, but you will if you hear.

Sam continued. "We made it past the number. That was the address on the house. That's the first line. We were going through the Violet Wood. That's the second line - the tallest lumber. We thought we'd figured out 'Whose name you found when only you hid', right?"

"Blythe," said Del.

"Right," said Sam. "The name you saw when you hid in the graveyard. That's the fourth line. But what about the third line of the riddle? What about 'Seek the one from whom under you slid?'"

"What about it?" asked Phil. "I don't even know what that means."

"What did we slide under to find the tombstone and the glass?" asked Sam.

"A hedge?" asked Del.

"We walked through hedges back in the forest!" Phil exclaimed. "Should we look for another one?"

"No, no. Do you remember what the priest called the hedge?" asked Sam. Del, Phil and Guy looked at him blankly. "I didn't either, but it came to me while you were arguing. He called it a thicket."

"So Mr. Thicket is in the riddle!" Guy declared.

"Exactly," said Sam. "And we met him in the right order. Mr. Thicket is line number three of the riddle. Old Blythe is line number four."

"What are you saying, Sam?" Phil asked.

"I'm saying that I think we should still be following the riddle, and I think that we were supposed to find Mr. Thicket before finding Old Blythe's cottage, and maybe Mr. Thicket is supposed to help us. When we find Old Blythe's cottage, the last two lines of the riddle will come in. Line five says the door will appear inside his fence. Line six says that we won't see if we look, but we will if we hear. That means that once we are there, we need to listen for something to find the door."

"Okay. First thing in the morning, we'll tell Mr. Thicket everything: the riddle, the priest, Old Blythe," said Phil.

"I don't think we should," said Del. "I don't care

what Sam says, I don't trust Mr. Thicket."

"We have to tell him something," said Phil. "He knows we're not telling him everything."

"We can just tell him that we've been told that there's a door to our world in or near Old Blythe's cottage, and we need help finding it," said Sam. "We don't need to tell him everything. If we act like we know what we're talking about, he'll probably think we know what we're talking about."

Del beamed at Sam. He wanted to get home and was willing to take Mr. Thicket's help, but he didn't trust him either. She realized they had very little choice. If they wanted to get home, they needed help, and right now, Mr. Thicket was it.

The four of them agreed that they wouldn't tell Mr. Thicket anything more. Then Guy, Sam, and Del went to their rooms so they could all get some sleep.

*****

Del had no idea what time of day it was when she awoke. When she had fallen asleep, there had been a lamp burning on a desk in the corner. Del figured it must have run out of fuel as her room was dark. There was one bit of light coming from a small crack under the door that led to the hallway. She figured it must be time to get up. She felt as though she had been asleep for days.

She got up and winced with the pain in her side. It had been feeling okay back on Hollow's boat, but ever since, it had been getting progressively worse.

She slowly made her way to the door, careful not to trip over or bump into anything on the way. She turned the handle of the door and pushed. Nothing. It was locked from the outside. She knew it! Mr. Thicket was evil, and they were his prisoners. Del wondered what she could do.

She didn't want to pound on the door or yell and scream - that would get her nowhere. She wanted to talk to her friends, to warn them. Maybe she could knock on a wall to communicate to Sam. She made her way to the wall. She tried to knock, but the walls were solid rock. There was no way she would be heard. Del started to panic. She wasn't terrified of the dark, but it is never a good feeling to be trapped in a dark room.

Then she heard a noise, like the shuffling of feet. Something was in her room with her. "Who's there?" she said. No answer, and no more shuffling. Del didn't know what to do. Then, in an instant, she made up her mind. She made a beeline for the door as quickly as she could, banged on it hard, and yelled at the top of her lungs "Help! Something's in here with me! Help! I'm locked in!"

Even with her voice at full volume, she could hear the footfalls coming toward her, this time fast. She braced for whatever would come next. Hands grabbed at her.

"Gotcha!" said Phil as the light from the lamp came back on. Guy stood by the desk controlling the lamp, but not controlling his laughter.

Close to tears, Del pushed Phil. "That was not funny."

Phil knocked on the door three times, and it swung open.

"C'mon Del, it was a little funny," Phil said, as Sam appeared on the other side of the door.

"You were in on this, too?" Del accused.

"We did get you pretty good," said Sam.

Del took the opportunity to knock the smaller and weaker Sam to the ground. She moved past him into the hall and stormed off.

Phil called to her, "Don't you want some breakfast? It was delivered by your lumen servant!" Guy stood next to Phil, holding a tray of food.

Del whipped around and glared at the boys. "No! I'm not hungry!" She turned back to continue storming off and bumped right into Mr. Thicket.

"You should really eat something, my dear. We have a big day ahead of us." He continued walking down the hallway and past their rooms.

*****

Del returned to her room and ate her breakfast while Phil, Guy, and Sam explained that they had already been up for quite some time making plans with Mr. Thicket.

"We're going to fly there!" said Guy.

"What?" said Del.

"The birds," Guy continued. "You know the birds that we saw in the hall, like the one Mr. Thicket rode in on to save us. He's going to let us ride them to Old Blythe's cottage."

"And... Mr. Thicket's coming with us," Phil said excitedly.

"Where did he go?" asked Del.

"Probably went to get the birds ready," Sam said.

"So, what happens when we get to the cottage?" said Del.

"Mr. Thicket just knows we need to find a magic door

in Old Blythe's yard," said Phil. "I say we ask him to go and talk to Old Blythe and distract him. Meanwhile, we sneak into the yard and listen to see if anything appears. If we find our way home, we'll go."

"And we won't come back," said Guy.

"And you think that'll work?" Del asked.

"It's all we've got," said Phil.

"What if we don't find the door right away?"

"Then we'll have to trust Mr. Thicket to get something out of Old Blythe. He must know what is in his own yard, and I'm sure the protector of Azdia is powerful enough to make Old Blythe tell us something."

"You're saying if we can't find it sneaking around, then Mr. Thicket will have to force Old Blythe to talk."

"I think it's the only way."

Del resigned herself to Phil's logic, though she wasn't convinced. "I guess you're right," she said.

"You done your food yet?" asked Guy, clearly excited to go flying.

Del nodded. The four of them left the room and headed toward the great hall where they had eaten their feast the night before.

*****

Phil and Guy ran up ahead of Sam and Del along the corridor. Sam was about to give chase, but Del held him back.

"Sam, I'm scared," she said.

"I think maybe we can trust him," said Sam.

"No, it's not that. It's this." Del winced with pain as she lifted the side of her shirt, revealing the large dark green bump and a mix of green and black vein-like streaks circling out from it across her skin. The vein streaks wrapped around to her back and her tummy.

"Del, how did this happen?" Sam asked.

"In the forest, on the first day here. Something stung me, I think. I kept thinking it would get better, and for a while on the boat, I thought maybe it was. But since the attack, since Crimson was carried off, it's hurt a lot more, and it's spreading."

"We've got to show the others," said Sam.

"No, I can't. Phil was there when I got stung, and he's forgotten about it. And Guy will just think I'm being a baby."

"No he won't. Del, this is bad. They'll think you're crazy for not saying anything earlier. We have to show them, and we have to show Mr. Thicket."

"No way. I don't trust him."

"I don't care whether you trust him or not. He rescued us, and he's agreed to help us. If he'd wanted to hurt us, he would have done it already. He may be able to make you better."

Del ran her hand over the bump, thinking. She knew Sam was right. She had been stupid to keep it secret this long, and she needed someone from this world to help her. What if dangerous Old Blythe attacked them and she got too sick to fight back? Or worse, what if they found the way back home and she left Azdia only to die from something that no human doctor could cure?

"Okay, I'll show them," said Del.

"Mr. Thicket, too?" asked Sam.

"Mr. Thicket, too."

Del and Sam walked along the corridors to the doors of the great hall to find Phil and Guy waiting outside.

"What took you so long?" said Phil.

"Phil wanted to wait for you guys to go in together," said Guy.

"We are in this together, right?" said Phil.

"Right," said Del.

Phil opened the doors.

*****

Five birds were waiting for them, each wearing a harness with reins hanging down. Mr. Thicket's cream-colored bird was back and among the five ready for the expedition. Del wondered whether it had attacked or just chased away the black winged creature.

Mr. Thicket rose from a seat at the table.

"Come, my children," he said. "There is no time to lose. Choose a bird, and let's be off."

"We can't," said Sam.

"What do you mean?" said Mr. Thicket.

"Del has something to show you all first," said Sam.

"What is it my dear?" asked Mr. Thicket.

Del lifted her shirt to reveal the mess of black and green.

"Holy!" said Guy.

Phil looked Del straight in the eyes. "Del, I'm so sorry. I had no idea it would get this bad."

"You knew?" said Guy.

Phil looked down. "Kind of," he said.

"It's okay, Phil," said Del. "It's not your fault. I should have shown the others on the boat, but I thought it was getting better then."

"Does it hurt?" said Guy.

"Yes," said Del. She looked at Mr. Thicket.

He knelt down next to her and said, "My dear,

everything is going to be okay."

"Can you help her?" Sam asked.

"Yes," said Mr. Thicket. "Do you remember being stung by something, Del?"

"Yes, but I don't know what it was. It was when we first arrived, so I didn't think much about it and kept thinking it would get better. Do you know what got me?"

"It is a particular kind of plant that stings when it feels threatened. The sting wards off attackers, but its after effects can be deadly. I need to put my hand on it, and it will hurt as I try to cure it."

"Okay," said Del.

Mr. Thicket put one hand on Del's shoulder and the other overtop of the dark green bump. "Ready?" he asked.

"Ready," Del said.

Mr. Thicket pressed on her side hard. Pain shot through Del's torso and down into her legs. She gritted her teeth but did not cry out. Flashes of green and black shot through the veins out from the lump. He released some pressure.

"Will that really do anything?" said Guy.

"The poison of the main wound must be disrupted," said Mr. Thicket. "While it is intact, it will keep feeding the body. The only way is to crush the main wound. Can you take a little more my dear?"

"I think so," said Del.

Mr. Thicket pressed hard again, and the green and black streaked across her back and tummy. Del fell forward under the pain. "That's enough," she panted, "I can't take anymore."

"You're okay," Mr. Thicket said. "I've broken the

main wound. It can no longer feed poison to the rest of your body."

Del's body didn't look any better.

"Do you hear that, Del?" said Phil. "You're going to be okay."

"Great," Del said, exhausted.

"It will take some time for your body to reject the rest of the poison, but you will start getting better," said Mr. Thicket. "We probably should go as soon as you feel up to it."

"I'll be okay in a few minutes," said Del.

*****

As soon as Del caught her breath and indicated she was ready to go, Phil and Guy climbed onto their birds: a fiery red one for Guy and a dark royal blue bird for Phil. Sam and Del were a little more tentative. They walked slowly toward the two remaining birds.

"Don't make me take the pink one," Sam said to Del.

"Just because I'm a girl, you think I should have to have pink?"

"No. But the guys won't let me hear the end of it if I have the pink one."

Del thought of Sam's role in the morning's practical joke, and without a way to get back at Guy and Phil, she raced for the green feathered bird, grabbed the reins, and hauled herself up.

"C'mon Del," Sam pleaded. "Let me have the green one. You know they picked the pink one for you!"

"I like this one. You take the pink one." Del replied.

"Hurry up children," Mr. Thicket called from his cream-colored bird. "Everyone ready yet?"

"Just a minute, Mr. Thicket," said Del. "Sam won't get on his bird."

"We're all waiting on you, Sam. Chop chop!" Mr. Thicket said.

"Ya. Chop chop, Sammy," said Guy. "Let's go already!"

"Oh, and… nice bird, man," said Phil.

Sam slowly lifted himself up and got seated. No sooner had he gotten up, the five birds were away. They circled the great hall twice, then zoomed single file up through a hole in the side of the cavern. It was dark in the tunnel - very dark. The birds picked up their pace. This was better than any roller coaster Del had ever been on. She held on tightly to the reins.

She could hear Sam behind her, "Oh no, oh no, oh no!" She knew there was nothing wrong. This was just what Sam did when he was on a fast ride. Guy was up ahead of Del, screaming. For all his bravery, he always had a high-pitched scream on the fast rides. Only Phil was silent, as Mr. Thicket chuckled to himself. Del figured he was laughing at the noises coming from the two boys. As they hurtled up and up, a pinprick of light appeared ahead. It got larger and larger until they burst through into glorious sunlight.

They were on their way to Old Blythe's Cottage.

CHAPTER NINETEEN

Old Blythe

Flying high above the Violet Wood on her green-feathered steed, Del let out a squeal of delight: "Whoo-hoo!" Then she shouted, "Guy, you were right! This is awesome!"

Guy looked a little sick as he clung to the reins and the neck of his bird.

Del looked below at the landscape. To their right, the forest continued as far as the eye could see. To their left was the end of the forest and the beginning of a vast plain, with smaller trees dotted here and there. A great herd of feldroes were loping across part of the plain.

Looking over her shoulder, Del could see a spectacular mountain range that stretched as far as her eyes could see. The closest mountain towered high above the other peaks. Near its top was the hole from which they had emerged. Del realized that Mr. Thicket's caverns were not just underground. They were inside that mountain as well. There had been many tunnels that they had not followed, many places inside that mountain that they had not explored.

They were moving away from the mountain range at a blistering speed. Del was shocked how quickly the birds could move through the air, especially as they carried people. She was loving every minute of the flight, and although the pain in her side continued, she managed to block it out of her mind as the wind rushed through her hair.

*****

After flying for a while, a steady plume of white smoke became visible on the horizon near the edge of the forest.

"Is that Old Blythe's Cottage?" Phil asked.

Mr. Thicket nodded and snapped the reins. The birds began their descent, not by slowing down, but by going into a steep dive. They swooped down and then along the tops of the trees, until finally, all five of them dropped into the forest and perched themselves in the high branches. The ride was over.

"We need to discuss our plan of attack," said Mr. Thicket.

Phil cut him off. "We were thinking that you could go knock on his door and distract him while we scope out the backyard."

Mr. Thicket laughed. "If Old Blythe saw me, he would know something is afoot. I have a much better plan."

Mr. Thicket furrowed his brow and leaned close to the children.

"Old Blythe sees everything that happens in his home and yard. So one of you must lure him away from his cottage while the others search for the door that will take you home. Del, you will be the best one to meet Old Blythe. He will believe you most easily. You will go knock on his door and tell him that you and your friends were in the forest and were attacked by terrible winged creatures. This is, of course, the truth. Now Old Blythe can be dangerous, but he never likes to see anyone in distress. He will want to help you. Tell him that your friends are injured and trapped under a fallen tree. If you tell him you need his help, he will go with you."

"I'm not sure I can do that," said Del.

"You can, my dear," said Mr. Thicket. "You are strong, and your friends need you. Old Blythe has no reason to doubt you."

"I don't think this is a very good idea," said Sam.

"Don't you worry," said Mr. Thicket. "I will be hidden in the trees keeping an eye on Del the whole time."

He pulled out a small pouch and tossed it to Phil. "Inside is a powder. When you find what you are looking for, throw the powder in Blythe's fireplace. It will change the color of the smoke from white to black. When I see it, I will get Del away from Old Blythe, and we will come to the cottage as fast as we can. Use the powder only if you have found your way back home. Do you understand?"

The children looked at each other, not knowing what to say. Del didn't feel great about being the bait for Old Blythe, but she understood why Mr. Thicket had chosen her. Sam wouldn't have had the confidence for this; Guy wouldn't have been able to think quickly enough if things changed on the fly; and Phil was needed to keep Sam and Guy on task in the all-important search. She had to be the one to meet Old Blythe.

*****

The birds descended from their perches in the treetops to the forest floor, allowing their riders to dismount. The four children did so, but Mr. Thicket remained on top of his bird.

"It will be easiest for me to watch everything from above," he said. "And I'll be able to take action more quickly this way."

Old Blythe's cottage was quaint. There was a white fence all around the well-maintained garden. The garden wasn't very big, but it was jammed packed with flowers, plants and shrubs. A path ran out of both the front and back gates. The cottage itself had ivy and moss growing on its grey stones, and it was capped with a thatched roof and a small red brick chimney.

All of them, including Mr. Thicket's bird, crept up to the side of the fence. There was no sign of anyone.

"This is it, my dear," said Mr. Thicket. "Remember I will be able to come to you quickly if there is a problem. Boys, as soon as Del and Old Blythe are clear, head through the fence and begin your search."

Mr. Thicket bent down from the bird and kissed Del on the forehead. "It is very important that you do not let Old Blythe see your side. He will use any perceived weakness to his advantage. But you are incredibly strong, my dear. Good luck!"

Del hugged each of her friends, even Guy. She could feel her heart pounding within her chest, and the pain in her side throbbed.

"We'll be home soon, Del," said Phil. "It'll work.

Don't worry."

"I know," Del said.

She walked straight toward the front path, then glanced back at the boys. The bird with Mr. Thicket took off and flew high into the trees. Knowing he was there, how he had rescued them before, and how he had helped treat her side, despite how much his treatment hurt, was a comfort to Del. She trusted him now. Mr. Thicket hadn't sugar-coated anything. He had told them the hard truth.

Del had wanted something better than the true story he had told them. She was in a fairytale world and wanted a fairytale ending, rather than a story that matched the harsh reality of Azdia. She wanted a better life, but Mr. Thicket could only present them with the real world where healing is painful and slow and where beliefs about what's good and bad, light and dark are muddled and confused. Now she knew to trust the one who told the truth even when the truth was hard. The one to believe was Mr. Thicket.

*****

There was no real security to the cottage. When Del reached the front gate, she simply reached through a hole and unlatched it, as easily as if she had been back home. She walked through the gate and took in the beautiful sights and smells of the garden. She had never seen so many and such a variety of flowers, all aglow with the inner light she had come to expect before entering the darker eighteenth province. Glowing butterflies danced from flower to flower. Caterpillars and other cute and colorful creepers crawled around on leaves and along the ground. There was a little bench over in the corner, well positioned to enjoy the garden. Del, drawn to it, found herself sitting on it, taking everything in.

Time seemed to stand still. She didn't think about home or the plan to deceive Old Blythe. She didn't think about much of anything for some time… until her eyes fell on the door to the cottage. The plan came flooding back to her. How long had she been sitting there? Everyone must be worried about her. She got moving, determined to carry out the plan.

She walked to the front door of the cottage and knocked. A few seconds later, the door swung open.

"Oh… uh… hello… hmm," a voice said. "Would you… um… like to…hmm… come in?"

Del didn't respond because the person she saw before her was so unexpected. Old Blythe was a small man with grey hair protruding out from under a soil-stained hat. He was not much taller than Del and was a little hunched over. He had an old, weathered face and wrinkly hands. He wore a tweed jacket and a collared shirt, covered by an apron.

"Are you…" Del hesitated, thinking that her question was about to sound really stupid. "Are you Old Blythe?"

The man chuckled. "Oh yes," he said, continuing to talk in a halting sort of way. "People do call me that… Do come in. I've got some… hmm… fresh muffins if you'd like."

The smell from inside the house wafted to Del's nostrils, tempting her to abandon the plan completely and simply agree to go in and have one.

"No," Del said, instead. "I'm in trouble and I need help. Me and my friends were attacked by these terrible things in the forest. I got away okay, but my friends got trapped under a big tree. The things flew away, and I tried to get the tree off them, but…"

"Now, slow down," Old Blythe said. "Let me get my other hat and… hmm… that walking stick of mine, and we'll go…um… have a look."

Old Blythe exchanged his hat for a different one, took off his apron, and grabbed an old knotted walking stick that was propped up in the entryway. He came outside and closed the door. He didn't lock it.

"Lead the way," he said.

That was easy, thought Del.

*****

The trick for Del was to keep a sense of urgency about finding her friends, but not stray too far from the cottage. She wanted to be able to keep the smoke from the chimney in her sights, so that if the boys discovered the way back home and changed the smoke from white to black, she would know it for herself. She decided to lead Old Blythe along the edge of the forest so that she could still see the cottage. She would be risking that he too would see the smoke, but now, after meeting him, she was confident that she could simply outrun him if it came to it. If she saw the smoke change color, she wouldn't wait for a rescue from Mr. Thicket; she would just take off back to the cottage and hopefully be home before Old Blythe could get anywhere near her.

"It's pretty far," Del said to Old Blythe. "We were in the forest, and I got out, then luckily walked this way and saw the smoke coming from your chimney. I'm glad someone was home."

"I'm almost always home," said Old Blythe.

They walked without speaking for some time. Old Blythe, though, never seemed to be perfectly silent. He whistled. He hummed. Often his whistling and humming were tuneless, but it all somehow made music. He'd take deep breaths and then let out all the air as a series of hums. His walk had a rhythm to it as well. No matter what Del did to take her mind off the humming and whistling and rhythm of the walking, she found herself smiling. She was somehow comforted by this strange, supposedly dangerous and possessive man. Whatever it was that Mr. Thicket had warned them about, she didn't really see it. Old Blythe just seemed a little quirky, but very likeable. Del was determined, however, to stick to the plan.

"You haven't told me your name, young lady," Old Blythe said.

"Oh, it's Del."

"Del is a very nice name," Old Blythe continued. "Is it short for something?"

"Delaney."

"Very beautiful, indeed. So, little Del, do you have any brothers or sisters?"

"Yeah, I have a sister."

"You aren't particularly happy about that fact are you?"

Del thought about the strange way that Old Blythe spoke. He halted over his words, yet each word seemed carefully chosen. He had a way of making you feel like you had to answer his questions. There was something about this that began to make Del think that Mr. Thicket was indeed right about how dangerous he could be.

She glanced over her shoulder. The smoke from the chimney was still white. She hoped the boys would find what they were looking for soon.

Bringing herself back to the conversation, Del said, "No, I don't like my sister. She doesn't like me either, so the feeling's mutual."

"What a shame. What happened between you to cause the disharmony?"

"Boys, mostly."

"Yes, they can be a problem."

"I know. It started with my mom, I guess. When my mom and dad split up, my sister started going out with older guys. They were the ones who made her meaner. Then when my mom started dating losers, my sister got even worse. When she has boy problems, she takes it out on me, and right now, she's with this guy who me and my friends call Jerk. I know it's not nice, but it's basically true."

"You miss them, though, don't you?"

Now how could he know that? thought Del. He cut right to the core of what she was really feeling with this one little question. Del felt compelled to answer. "Yes."

"It's okay," Old Blythe said. "We'll find your friends and get them out from under that tree; then you can be on your way home to your mother and sister."

"I hope so," Del said, and she really meant it. She really did want to go home to her mom and, yes, even to her sister.

She looked over her shoulder. The cottage was very far away now as they had been walking for some time. She could still see the outline of the roof and the thinnest trail of grey smoke floating up. Grey smoke. Or was it white? They kept walking and Del kept checking over her shoulder. Never once did Old Blythe look back. Although he was clearly able to sense Del's deepest longings for home, Old Blythe seemed oblivious to Del's nervous backward glances. He was a strange sort of man.

The smoke was getting darker. It was definitely not white. It was slowly turning black. This was it. She was not going to wait for a rescue from Mr. Thicket. Del was going to make a run for it, back to the cottage as fast as she could, hoping that the boys had found the way back home.

Del stopped, turned toward Old Blythe and said, "I'm sorry." Then she tore as fast as she could back toward the cottage. She didn't look back to see if Old Blythe was chasing her. She just kept her eyes fixed on the now fully black smoke billowing up above the outline of the cottage roof.

CHAPTER TWENTY

Nothing Is What It Seems

Del had covered about half the distance back to the cottage when she saw Mr. Thicket's bird swoop out of the trees. He landed just outside the cottage gate, dismounted quickly, and went inside. For the first time in her run, Del looked over her shoulder and was surprised to see that Old Blythe was walking toward her and the cottage at the same rhythmic pace he had previously kept when they had walked and talked together. She felt a pang of guilt for lying to him but tried to put that out of her mind. If she could get home, it would be worth it, and she figured that Old Blythe was probably more dangerous than she thought. She kept up her pace, anxious to see her friends and get home, if they had indeed been successful.

Del arrived at the already open gate to the cottage and took a look back. Old Blythe was around the halfway mark. If her friends had not found the way back home, they would still have enough time to manage an escape. She passed through the gate.

"Sam!" Del cried.

Sam glanced her way and just before disappearing through a shimmering oval of light, he shouted back to her, "Del, we did it!"

A beam of light fed the oval light-door. Del's eyes followed the beam down to a glass. It looked just like the one she'd found in the graveyard. They had done it. She wasn't sure how they had found it, but Del didn't care. After days, or more like weeks, she was going home. She was even happy about seeing her sister. She knew that when she arrived home, her mom would be more relieved and thankful than angry; at least, deep down she would be. Del would need to come up with a story for why she had been gone so long, but in the end, she just knew that everything would be okay in her family. Del's longed-for embrace from her mother was only a few minutes away.

Next to the glass and oval stood Mr. Thicket smiling. Del ran over to him. "Did they all go through?" she asked.

"They did," Mr. Thicket replied. "I told them there was no time, that they would need to go through right away and that I would get you through after."

"Good thinking," Del said as she moved toward the oval. "We'll always be grateful for your help, Mr. Thicket."

Mr. Thicket moved to block Del's path.

"That's not a very good goodbye now, is it?" he said. "You're not like the other three, my dear. Only you were able to go out there with Old Blythe. Only you were able to keep up the ruse with him."

"I thought you said we have no time. I've got to go home," Del insisted.

Mr. Thicket ignored her plea, stood his ground, and

continued. "Only you were able to lie like that because you are deceitful, and this is a trait that I find very... valuable. You're more resilient than the others. Your heart is not easily swayed, but I don't need more easily swayed hearts. I can use someone passionate, someone who can do whatever it takes. Someone who can meet Old Blythe and still lie to him. Someone who can pass that test."

Del's head was swimming again, on the edge of passing out. What was going on?

"Let me through," she said as she tried to push past Mr. Thicket.

He grabbed her by the arm, and she felt instantly cold.

Without letting go of Del, Mr. Thicket bent down and picked up the glass. The oval of light disappeared, and a sickening smile crossed Mr. Thicket's face.

"Now I have everything I came for," he said.

"What are you doing?" Del questioned. "Who are you?"

"Don't worry, my dear," said Mr. Thicket. "You'll have all the answers you need in time. I promise; no harm will come to you in the end."

Del felt nauseous and faint. Her side seethed with pain, and the place where Mr. Thicket's fingers locked around her arm burned with cold. She summoned what little strength she had left and tried to pull away from Mr. Thicket. It was no use. He pulled her toward the gate as though she were a rag doll.

"We're going, my dear, and I am leaving with what will be my two prize possessions." Del knew that he meant the glass and her.

How had this all happened? She couldn't understand

how the lumens could honor this horrible man. How could the savior of Azdia be so cruel?

"Why won't you let me go home?" Del cried.

"You are far more useful to me than I had originally thought, my dear," Mr. Thicket replied. "And besides, I saw it in your face when you came into the garden. Old Blythe got to you. I knew right away your trust for me had eroded even if it was just a bit. Whatever seed that he sowed in you will only grow if you go home now. You'll convince your friends that he is the good one, and I am not. You'll return to Azdia, and that will signal my defeat. But if I keep you here with me, you'll either be turned to see my truth, or you will be locked away where no one will ever find you. Either way, when your friends return to look for you, whether it's in a year, ten years, or a hundred years, I will be ready for them."

Del's heart sank. She only hoped that Old Blythe would be back fast enough to help her although she had no idea what he could do to stand up to the power of Mr. Thicket. They left the garden, and Del could see by his slow pace that Old Blythe would not make it in time. All hope was gone. They had believed in Mr. Thicket, but now she knew that he was the evil one. They had all been deceived, and she had become the prisoner of a madman.

*****

Del struggled, attempting to free herself, but the icy grip of her captor was too strong, and her nausea overwhelmed her. Radiating from the place where his fingers met her arm was a horrible dark green color, running across and under her skin. Del was revolted as she looked at it and thought about what Mr. Thicket had done to her to "heal" the wound on her side. She knew now that he had not healed it, but added to it in some way, making it much worse.

As they made their way from the gate to the cream-colored bird, Mr. Thicket, like Del, kept his eyes on Old Blythe who never quickened his pace. It was as if he didn't see them at all. Del wondered whether somehow Mr. Thicket had made them invisible, or perhaps Old Blythe just didn't care about the scene in front of his cottage.

They reached the bird, and Mr. Thicket placed the glass into one of the pouches attached to its harness. He grabbed the reins in one hand and prepared to swing himself and Del up to fly away.

He never let his gaze move from Old Blythe, and this, it turned out, was his undoing. Because while Old Blythe was too far away to do anything about the escape, neither Del nor Mr. Thicket saw what came from behind, out of the garden.

Mr. Thicket was tackled by a lumen. His grip broke from Del. She threw up instantly, and intense pain stabbed in her side, her stomach, and her arm where Mr. Thicket's fingers had been. She fell to the ground, barely able to move. The dark green, accompanied by the terrible burning cold, now covered her arm, and had begun to invade the rest of her body. She felt as though she was changing from the outside in. What was she becoming? Was it some terrible creature of darkness? Was this what Mr. Thicket did to lumens to remove their light?

Between the stabs of pain and the cold, she crawled toward the garden gate, feeling like there may be some safety closer to the cottage. The lumen attacker had knocked Mr. Thicket down and was trying to pin him to the ground. Mr. Thicket bumped his assailant off and headed straight for the pouch that contained the glass. Before he could get there, the lumen jumped on him again, knocking Mr. Thicket to his knees. The lumen did everything he could to stop Mr. Thicket from reaching the pouch, but it wasn't enough.

With the lumen on his back punching and scratching, Mr. Thicket opened the pouch and retrieved the glass. He flipped the lumen off his back. A kind of green lightning flew out of the glass and struck the lumen, sending him flying through the air, hitting the fence. His limp body lay a few feet from Del.

Del's tunnel vision continued. She gazed at the lumen who had tried in vain to save her and was convinced that it was Crimson. But that couldn't be, could it? Perhaps she was hallucinating. She reached out to him and grabbed his hand. At his touch, the pain in Del's arm and side subsided a bit, and the spread of the green slowed. Del, however, braced for the next blow from Mr. Thicket, which was sure to be fatal.

The lumen's eyes fluttered open. They danced and flickered.

"Don't worry, Del," he whispered. "Mr. Thicket will save us."

Del figured that he must have been more delirious than she.

*****

The fatal blow of green lightning never came. Del's mind raced trying to make some sense of what had just happened, but thinking was useless while her tunnel vision persisted. She kept her hand clasped around the lumen's hand, and somehow, despite everything, she felt better.

"Look," said the lumen.

Del craned her neck a little bit to see that Old Blythe had finally arrived.

"You've been busy," Old Blythe said to Mr. Thicket.

"And you've been doing nothing as usual," came the reply. "This time, you have paid the price."

"If you mean the crystal seed, I cannot allow you to leave with it. You will need to give it back."

"Your power is fading, old man. You won't be able to stop what I've put in motion. You are too late."

Old Blythe held out his hand. "The seed, if you please."

Mr. Thicket produced the glass and sent green lightning hurtling toward Old Blythe. Rather than being hit by it, however, Old Blythe's outstretched hand caught hold of the lightning. It didn't dissipate. If anything it grew stronger, less green, and much brighter. Old Blythe smiled a knowing smile, cocked his head in Del's direction, and gave her a wink. Calmly and mischievously, he pulled on the lightning as though it was a rope in a tug of war, hand over hand. Mr. Thicket, at a loss for what to do, refused to let go of the glass and was pulled along with it toward Old Blythe. The closer he got to Old Blythe, the more panicked be became.

"You really ought to just give me the crystal seed, you know," said Old Blythe. "You really should just let go. You know in a moment you will have to."

Once the two men were close to each other, Mr.

Thicket pulled back hard on the glass, lifted his arm up, and threw the glass as hard as he could at Old Blythe. Mr. Thicket turned and ran back to his bird as Old Blythe quite easily caught the glass in one hand. The lightning recoiled back into it.

Mr. Thicket swung up onto his bird and took off. Del watched in amazement as the protector of Azdia, who had deceived them all, left without her and without the glass. She could not believe what had just happened. She could not believe the strength of Old Blythe. He now possessed the glass that could take her home. There was still a chance for her.

"Now where did I leave that walking stick?" Old Blythe said. He looked around and found it lying on the ground. "There we go." He walked over toward Del and spoke to her. "You left in a hurry. I supposed your friends in the woods managed to help themselves, did they?"

Del, ashamed, didn't know what to say.

Old Blythe continued, "Don't you worry, little Del. Your friends are indeed safe and sound back home where they belong. And you will join them soon enough. First you need some rest to prepare for the journey. Looks like your friend Crimson here could use a little more tending to as well. Let's get you both indoors."

Del's mouth dropped open in disbelief. Old Blythe knew the boys had gone through the light-oval? This really was Crimson lying next to her? Perhaps the nightmare was over. Old Blythe was promising to send her home. There was hope. Perhaps her mouth wasn't open in disbelief. Perhaps it was open in awe and in a spark of belief. Perhaps Del had found faith, or more accurately, someone worthy of her faith.

"And I think the word you are looking for is 'sorry'," said Old Blythe as he helped the two of them to their feet.

Del was about to say the word, but as soon as Del rose, her head swam more, the world spun a few times, and the tunnel vision got instantly worse until all she could see was a pinprick of light.

Del collapsed on the ground and heard a distant voice say, "I think she's getting worse." It was Crimson.

Just before she blacked out completely, she heard the other voice, Old Blythe's voice. "But for the first time in a long time, she's about to get better."

CHAPTER TWENTY-ONE

The Crystal Seed

Del awoke and found herself wrapped in blankets in a very cozy bed in a very cozy room. She decided that she felt so comfortable that she never wanted to leave that bed. She felt unbelievably good - better than her very first day in Azdia - perhaps better than she had ever been. Crimson sat next to her in a big easy chair, quietly reading a book.

"How long was I out?" Del asked.

"Oh! You're awake," said Crimson. "It's hard to know. You slept for some time. You're looking a lot better."

"I feel great!" said Del. "I never want to leave this bed, though. Except I'm hungry."

"That's a good sign. I'll go get some soup."

Before Del could stop him to ask the thousand questions in her head, Crimson scurried off through the door.

Del looked around to take in her surroundings. The room was cluttered with all kinds of things, most of them looking not particularly like they were from Azdia, but from various places on earth. She had learned about China and Japan at school and immediately recognized pieces of what must have been old Chinese or Japanese pottery, with figures of dancing dragons on them. In one corner of the room, there was an old looking bicycle, the kind with a giant front wheel. On a desk near the window sat an odd looking, blue-colored, see-through television, or maybe an old style of computer, shaped like a teardrop. On the walls hung beautiful art. The room was jammed full of mismatched decorations, furniture, and trinkets, but somehow the atmosphere was calming despite the clutter. Del remembered that Old Blythe liked to collect things.

As she strained to remember exactly what happened with Mr. Thicket, Old Blythe, and Crimson, Del suddenly realized that she was not in any pain. She pulled back her covers and lifted her shirt. The veins had shrunk, and the black and dark green had faded. She ran her hand over her side. The bump was still there, but smaller. It was still a little tender, but by no means did it hurt the way it had.

She covered herself back up as Crimson reappeared carrying a tray with two bowls of soup, bread, and water. He placed it on the desk, next to the strange looking TV-computer.

"I figured I'd have some too. It smelled so good," he said.

Del got out of bed and was dizzy for a second or two. She steadied herself and took a seat at the desk with Crimson. She grabbed a slice of bread and started eating. It tasted wonderful.

"Aren't you forgetting something?" Crimson said. Del

looked at him, and Crimson was holding his glass of water up, asking her to toast Mr. Thicket.

"You're not serious!" Del exclaimed. "I'll never do that again as long as I live. Not after what he did!"

"After what he's done, this is the very least we can do," Crimson shot back. "There's no way we can repay him for all his goodness to us. This is just a gesture. We thank him for everything. For our freedom, our food, and, I mean, he literally made this food downstairs!"

"What on earth are you talking about?"

"Del, we're in Mr. Thicket's house. Mr. Thicket, who saved both of us. I thought you would remember, but maybe you've blocked it out. Maybe the sickness took more out of you than we'd thought. Do you remember the man with the bird?"

"Crimson - the man with the bird is Mr. Thicket."

"No, no, no, no, no," Crimson laughed. "Mr. Thicket is the old man who caught the lightning. The other man, the one with the bird was but a rumour until now. Now we know who we're up against. The man with the bird, the one who hurt you is Mordlum's heir."

"I'm so confused," said Del. "The man with the bird rescued us in the forest after you were... well... we thought you were..."

"Dead," said Crimson. "I know. I did too, believe me."

"Anyway," said Del, "The bird man told us that he was Mr. Thicket. He was helping us get home, that is until I got here and he went crazy."

"He was lying to you, Del. That's what he does. He's not Mr. Thicket, but I'm shocked that even he would try to pull off impersonating him. Rumours have been going around that Mordlum's heir - he's a descendant of the original evil one - is the one behind the growing darkness."

"So what about 'Old Blythe?'" asked Del. "This is Blythe's cottage after all. Remember - that's where we were heading when we set out through the Violet Wood."

"I don't know," said Crimson.

"What do you mean you don't know?" asked Del.

"I remember being attacked by that thing in the forest, then I woke up here. Mr. Thicket told me I was asleep for quite some time, and that I needed a fair amount of mending to get me back to my normal self. The first time I had left his house was when I saw you were in trouble. So, I don't know anything about finding Old Blythe."

"So, you didn't see the boys?" Del asked.

"No. I think I must have been asleep." Crimson replied.

"Crimson, this is Old Blythe's cottage!"

"No - it is Mr. Thicket's house!" Crimson said.

"It can't be both places, unless..." Del tried to put things together in her mind.

"Unless he hasn't yet been properly and fully introduced to either of you." It was Old Blythe bounding through the door. "I do apologize for the confusion. Allow me to tell you the full truth and my full name. I am Blythe Thicket."

Del and Crimson looked confused, then looked at each other and smiled.

"You're the same person?" Del said, "You've always been the same person?"

"Think about the riddle, little Del," said Blythe Thicket.

"You know about the riddle?" Del asked.

"Of course I do," said Blythe Thicket. "Listen to the lines again. 'Seek the one from whom under you slid / Whose name you found when only you hid.' "

"We thought that meant we were supposed to find Thicket first because we had slid under a bush or a thicket back in the graveyard. Then find Blythe because that was the name on the tombstone."

"Ah, I can see how that would make sense. Except it was simpler than that. The lines were giving you one description of a single person - Blythe Thicket. You were given the Thicket name first, because it is that name that all of Azdia knows. You were given Blythe second because, in these parts, people know me merely as Old Blythe."

Del sat puzzling.

"You really should eat some soup, little Del," said Blythe Thicket. "You have done so well through this whole ordeal, and now you need to gain back your strength. Something you have in spades."

Del took her spoon in her hand, then slowly laid it back down. She looked at Blythe Thicket a little suspiciously. Then with a smirk, she grabbed her water glass, lifted it to the sky and cried aloud, "To Mr. Thicket!" It felt so incredibly good to say those words.

Blythe Thicket leaped in the air in delight. "Now you've got it, little Del! Now we are getting somewhere!"

From nowhere, a goblet appeared in his hand as he danced around the room.

"Today I toast to you, as you have toasted me." Blythe Thicket was brimming with excitement and glee as he half spoke, half sang. "Though she may be small today, her strength will many foes allay. She wields her wits alone to stand against the darkness of our land. We look to the time of growing light, when she returns to lead the fight."

Blythe Thicket paused, ran over to the window, opened it, and shouted, "To little Del!"

Crimson stood up with his glass in hand. "To Del and Mr. Thicket!"

Del, bewildered, but filled with joy, ran her hand over her side. The bump was gone.

*****

Del spent the next few days recovering. She explored the rest of the cottage and found that each room was full of trinkets much like her room. It seemed that the heir of Mordlum was telling the truth about one thing - Old Blythe loved to collect things. Blythe Thicket would disappear for hours at a time, and while he was away, Del would think of questions to ask him. What is the plan to defeat Mordlum's heir? Why is all the stuff you've collected from earth? How did you get it? Where did you come from? When can I go home? These were all questions she readily asked Crimson, but he had no answers. Strangely, when Blythe Thicket returned to the cottage, all of Del's questions seemed to fade away.

Blythe Thicket had a way of controlling the conversation and for the entire time Del was in his home, he kept the talk very light. Each day over the evening meal, he would tell stories that seemed to have no point to them, he would tell jokes, he would talk about a single flower that he had seen that day growing in the forest and how wonderful it was. Following the meal, he would get out a board game or a deck of cards and ask Del and Crimson to play. They had fun together. They simply enjoyed each other's company.

Del had a fantastic time at Blythe Thicket's cottage. She lost all track of time, much like she had aboard the Zephyr. She could easily have been there weeks or possibly even months. To her, it always felt like just a day or two, but in her mind, she knew it must have been longer.

*****

On a particular day, following their supper, Old Blythe did not invite Del and Crimson to play a game. Instead, he cleared his throat and looked rather serious.

"Little Del, the time has come for you to return home."

Del hadn't thought about home in a long time. She wasn't sure if she was excited or nervous. Suddenly, she felt terribly guilty for not thinking of home the whole time she had been in Blythe Thicket's house.

"Don't feel bad for spending time here with me and not thinking of home, little Del," said Blythe Thicket, reading her mind. "This rest has done you a world of good, and it was something you needed. Take a look at your side."

Del had never shown Blythe Thicket her side, nor talked about it with him. She wondered at how he knew, but then realized that he knew everything. She lifted her shirt and saw her perfect skin. There was no sign that anything had ever been wrong.

Del marvelled at how Blythe Thicket did things and how different he was than the heir of Mordlum. She not only trusted Blythe Thicket, she loved him with all her heart. It was a pure love, as though he were her grandfather and she his only grandchild. She knew in her mind that Blythe Thicket cared about everyone, but in her heart, it felt like he loved her best. She imagined that everyone who really knew Blythe Thicket felt the same way about him.

"I think you'll find, when you return, that you will have changed," Blythe Thicket said. "But everyone else will barely notice. You will wonder why everyone is the way they are because you have been through so much. The truth is, they have not had the adventures you have had, and they don't know me quite the way you do."

"But, won't they all have been terribly worried?" Del asked.

Blythe Thicket avoided the question and instead started looking around his cluttered living room. "Now where did I put it?" he said to himself. "Ah, yes. Here it is." He held out the glass.

"I'm going now?" Del asked.

"Yes," Blythe Thicket replied. "But first you must know a few things for when you return to Azdia."

"I'm going to return?"

"But of course you are," said Blythe Thicket. "You are little Del, the chief of the Malak."

"I'm what?"

"Search your heart, and think over the time you've spent here with me in this cottage. Do you not know this to be true about yourself by now?"

"But, we just joked around, listened to stories, and played games," Del replied.

"Look deeper," Blythe Thicket said.

Del tried to look deeper, but she couldn't seem to do

it.

"It will come, in time," said Blythe Thicket. "You will see it, even if you don't see it now. But it is time to get you home. And before you go, you must know something about this seed, and about the one in your world."

"Seed?" Del asked, looking intently at the glass in Blythe Thicket's hand.

As he spoke, light swirled within the glass. "This is a crystal seed, as is the one you found near the Blythe stone. When the crystal seeds come together into one, they have great and powerful magic. But when darkness first came to Azdia, it became necessary to hide the seeds since the powers of darkness sought to use them for evil. I kept them separate and decided to hide one in your world close to some friends."

"The priest," Del said.

"Yes, and his wife," said Blythe Thicket. "Hiding a seed in your world was one of my more clever tricks. I made it so that the only way to get from your world to this one is through the bridge created by the crystal seed next to the Blythe stone. There is no easy way to bring the seed from your world back here once the bridge is open because it is impossible to carry a seed through its own bridge."

"So, how did you get the seed into the graveyard in the first place?" Del asked.

"Ahh, that would be giving away quite a secret now, wouldn't it?" said Blythe Thicket. "Back in the dark times, Mordlum believed he had found a way to bring the crystal seeds together. And now I fear his heir, in making a move for my seed, may have discovered how to do it as well."

"Why don't you just destroy the seeds?" asked Del.

"The seeds have powerful magic, and any attempt to destroy them would have terrible effects on Azdia. It should not be tried." Blythe Thicket answered. "Little Del, our best hope in this dark time is to keep the crystal seeds hidden. Then when the time is right, they can be used for the good of both our worlds."

Blythe Thicket leaned close to Del and whispered to her. "Little Del, you will return to Azdia to lead the lumens against the darkness. But when you do return, like Eleanor before you, you cannot stay forever. You must know how to find a seed to get home."

"Why couldn't I just come here and be with you? You'd be able to send me home."

"The heir of Mordlum knows my seed is here, and the darkness in this province grows and grows. By the time you return, this seed and I will be far from here. There are other seeds, however. With the right key, you will be able to find one of them for your future journey home.

"How many seeds are there?"

"Suddenly, you are full of questions, Little Del. Let's worry about all the seeds another day. For now, you need only to know how to find one. You will need to remember a new riddle."

Blythe Thicket looked very serious as he recited:
Old Blythe signed next to this one's name;
Trust her completely, despite her fame.
Over the sea where the new birth falls,
Choose the tunnel or scale the walls.
When you arrive at the desert's edge
And stand looking out from the highest ledge,
The sun will touch the place you must go;

And there will you see the ominous glow.
You'll find what you need by looking below.

"But what does it mean?" Del asked.

"I cannot reveal its secret to you," said Blythe Thicket. "If you were to just know the location of the seed you must find, and if you were captured, you could be forced to tell them. If all you know is the riddle, it is far safer. What I can tell you is that when you are home, you will need to go inside the old church and look through a book that deals with birth, death, and marriage. Don't forget that, as it is the key."

"Why so cryptic?" Del asked again.

"There are people in your world who cannot be trusted," said Blythe Thicket. "You must be on your guard. Now, do you have the riddle in your mind?"

"No, not at all," Del stammered. "I wish Sam were here. He's great at remembering these kinds of things."

"It would have been good if Samuel had stayed. He is trustworthy and kind." said Blythe Thicket. "But don't worry - we'll just keep repeating it until you've got it."

And they did. Even Crimson got in on the repeating until he too, along with Del were singing the words of the riddle, having no real idea what the words meant. As with most things in Blythe Thicket's cottage, learning the riddle became fun.

*****

After countless repetitions, Blythe Thicket stopped the singing and held the crystal seed in his palm.

"It's time," he said, and he placed the seed on the floor. A beam of light shone up and displayed the oval of light: the entry to the bridge leading home.

Del ran into Blythe Thicket's arms. "Thank you," she said.

"My little Del," said Blythe Thicket. "It has been a pleasure."

After her embrace with Blythe Thicket, Del stood looking at Crimson. Tears streamed down her face. She had been through a lot with him, and after all of her longing for home, now that it came to it, she was not keen on going. A big part of that was the cottage and Blythe Thicket's presence, but face to face with Crimson, she realized that she cared for him deeply, and this might be her last time seeing him.

"Can't he come with me?" she asked.

Blythe Thicket shook his head.

"It has been an honour to walk side by side with you, my lady," Crimson said. He bowed low as if she were royalty.

"Don't you call me anything but Del," said Del. They walked toward each other and gave each other a long hug. Del never wanted to let go.

"You need to go home, Del," said Crimson. "I wish I could come with you. But, you will return to Azdia, and I will find you when you do."

"But how?" asked Del.

"I just will," said Crimson. "Now go."

He ended their hug, and, holding her by the hand, led her over to the oval of light.

"Goodbye little Del," said Old Blythe.

"Goodbye," Del sobbed.

She stepped into the oval, and all went black.

CHAPTER TWENTY-TWO

Will They Return?

Del fell out of the nothingness of the bridge connecting the worlds onto the patch of grass next to the tombstone. She fully expected to be alone after spending so long at Blythe Thicket's cottage, but everyone was there: Phil, Guy, Sam, even the priest and his wife.

"You took your time," Phil joked.

"What are you all doing here?" said Del. "Do you come here every day?"

"Time kind of stands still while you're on the other side," said Guy.

"Mostly," said Sam. "It seems you can be there for days and only minutes will go by here."

The reality of what this meant sunk in. Del realized that it was still the same Saturday as when they first dug out what they thought was a magic stone, but in reality was one of the crystal seeds of Azdia.

"My sister and her boyfriend!" Del panicked. They had been on their way to the graveyard, intending to intrude on what they were doing that day.

"We sent them away," the priest's wife said. "It was easy enough. None of you were here, and that was clear. The two of them seemed quite impatient and ran off."

"Guys, I'm dying to know how you found the glass stone," said Del, deciding not to call it by its right name.

"We're dying to know why it took you so long to get here," said Sam.

"You guys go first 'cause you're not going to believe my story."

"It wasn't that hard really," said Phil. "We figured because the riddle mentioned Old Blythe's fence, that it was probably in the garden somewhere. All we had to go on was that we would see something when we could hear something. So, we walked around the garden listening for who knows what. We kept calling to one another 'I don't hear anything.' Then Sam had the idea that in order to really hear something we couldn't call back and forth or move because every time we made noise it would make it hard to hear. So the three of us stood perfectly still. Guy kept asking if he could move or speak yet, and we'd have to start over."

"It felt like forever just standing there listening," said Guy.

"Anyway," Phil continued. "Eventually we stood for long enough, and we started to hear something. We said nothing to each other; we just kept listening."

"What did you hear?" Del asked.

"We heard Mrs. Manters ask Reverend Manters if he wanted more tea," said Sam.

"What?" said Del.

"We could hear the conversation going on in the clearing right here," said Phil. "We could hear it in Old

Blythe's garden. Then we just followed the sound of the voices and found the glass stone. That's when Guy ran into the house to change the smoke of the chimney and give you the signal. Sam and I activated the glass and the light oval appeared. We were waiting for you when Mr. Thicket came back. He told us to go through right away because there wouldn't be a second to lose. We needed to go through so that he could get you out quickly. When you didn't come through right after us, we knew something must have happened."

"It's too long of a story to tell right now, and..." Del began.

She thought for a moment, and decided that it would be better to tell the story when the four of them were by themselves, without the priest or his wife around.

"It's not important," she continued. "The important thing is we're all home safe and sound."

"Maybe we should all head home," Sam said. "It's really only been a few hours, but it feels like weeks."

Everyone crawled out of the clearing.

"You children must keep this place secret," said Mrs. Manters. "Mr. Manters and I will continue to protect the bridge. It will be here for you to return to Azdia."

"We're not going back," said Phil. "That place was too crazy."

Del locked eyes with Mrs. Manters and nodded as if to say, "I'll be going back." Mrs. Manters and her husband both nodded knowingly back to Del.

*****

The four friends left the churchyard and walked along the familiar lane. Del knew she needed to tell the boys about the real Blythe Thicket, about Crimson being alive, and about how the man that had rescued and helped them was actually the heir of Mordlum. She tried to tell them everything, but things came out kind of scrambled as she packed what could easily have been an hour long story into all of thirty seconds.

When she had finished, her friends were silent for a while. Then Phil spoke up. "So you're saying the man who rescued us, the man who gave us the best food, and the man who helped us find the cottage and the glass stone so we could get home is really the most evil man in Azdia?"

"Yes, but…" Del stammered, "I'm not telling it very well. He lied to us about being Mr. Thicket. Old Blythe is Mr. Thicket. The one we thought was Mr. Thicket is actually the heir of Mordlum, and he wasn't going to let me come home. He was going to capture me."

"I'm sorry, Del, but none of this seems right," said Phil. "Mr. Thicket warned us that Old Blythe would probably lie to you, and you'd come back telling a crazy story."

"You have to believe me," Del pleaded. "I'm telling the truth. The heir of Mordlum is evil, and the one you know as Old Blythe needs our help to stop him. We have to go back to Azdia and fight against the darkness."

"Think about what you are saying," said Phil. "We all met Mr. Thicket. We all trusted him. And now you're asking us to believe he's the bad guy and that we should go back to that crazy place and fight him?"

"Phil's right," said Guy. "I liked Mr. Thicket. When we left, he said he would get you home too, Del. And here you are safe and sound."

"Why don't you guys believe me? I had weeks, maybe months in Blythe Thicket's cottage, and it was incredible! It totally changed everything about how I feel about Azdia, and I know that I have to go back."

"Go back then," said Phil. "But we're not going with you."

The friends had arrived at the front walk to Del's house. They stopped. She had been dreaming of a reunion with her mother after weeks of being apart, and while Del still felt home sick, she now knew that her mother wouldn't feel any differently about her. Del's heart sank. She had only been gone a few hours.

"Let's not fight, guys," she said. "It's not worth it."

"You're right, Del," said Phil. "We can figure this all out later."

"Shoot," said Sam as he motioned along the street. "Here comes Jerk and his girlfriend."

*****

Del swung around. Normally, she would have initiated a detour through her yard and out the back gate, away from her sister and Jerk, but actually seeing Suzanne, she didn't want to. A lump formed in her throat, and she held back tears of joy at the sight of her sister. This was unexpected. She knew that she had missed her mom, but her sister? Her feelings faded when Suzanne opened her mouth.

"You're a little sneak, aren't you?" Suzanne said. "Guess you didn't go to the church to marry your three boyfriends after all."

"Wow, she's gonna cry before we even get going this time," said Jerk.

"Not today, okay guys." Sam tried to stand up for Del a little.

"Shut up, infant." Jerk said.

"You were supposed to take us with you this morning," Suzanne continued. "What happened to our little plan? Our little agreement?"

"There was no agreement," said Del.

"Oh, I think there was," said Suzanne. "The agreement was that we'd come with you to the churchyard to see whatever you had found."

Guy and Phil tried to make themselves bigger and positioned themselves between Del and Suzanne.

"Let's just go, Del," said Sam, pulling on her arm.

"You're a smart one, Deli." Suzanne kept going. "Three boyfriends are better protection for you. Especially, this one." She ran her hand up and down Guy's arm, and he turned a deep shade of pink.

Suzanne looked right at Phil and Guy. "What are you two doing hanging out with these losers, anyway? You guys are cooler than that." Guy turned from pink to red.

Jerk just laughed as the four friends shuffled away from them along the sidewalk. Suzanne called after Del, "You gotta come home sometime. And when you do, you're gonna get it. I know you moved my phone this morning. Don't you ever touch it again! That's my private property!"

Del sobbed as she walked.

"I hate those two," Sam said.

"I actually don't," Del said. "She's my sister. I missed her so much. Sam, can I come to your place? I'm not ready to see my mom just yet."

"Sure," Sam said.

The four friends arrived at the corner of Elm Avenue and Fife Street. Sam's place lay in one direction while Guy and Phil needed to go the other way to get to their houses.

"Listen, Del," said Phil. "Something happened to you in Azdia that didn't happen to us. You got sick, and we didn't, y'know. Mr. Thicket did what he could to make you better, but maybe... I don't know, I'm just saying, that maybe you imagined some stuff that didn't happen. Maybe you dreamed some stuff with Crimson and Old Blythe. Maybe with you being sick, maybe you thought some things happened that didn't actually happen."

"I know what was real," Del said, but even as she said the words, she doubted a little. It was possible that Phil was right. She might have dreamt it all. She had been back less than an hour, and already memories of Blythe Thicket's cottage were beginning to fade.

"I'm just saying," said Phil, "that it's possible that you imagined some stuff. That's all."

"Okay, Phil," Del conceded. She didn't want to argue and she knew this was his way of settling things. She walked over and gave him a hug, remembering how when they had first entered Azdia that he had saved her life with some pretty powerful words. She had felt so close to Phil then and knew their relationship had strengthened because of that time together.

She hugged Guy, too, but said nothing. He was a dear friend, but they wouldn't usually hug. She did it anyway because it seemed like the right thing to do. Then she and Sam walked in the direction of Sam's house, and Phil and Guy went the other way.

Del was disappointed. No plan had been hatched; no scheme had been plotted. They hadn't even made plans to meet the next day.

*****

Del and Sam arrived at Sam's house and went inside.

"Mom?" Sam called.

"In the kitchen," a voice called back.

Sam ran to the kitchen with Del close behind. Upon arriving, he ran to his mother and threw his arms around her.

"I missed you, mom," Sam said. "And I love you."

"I love you too, Sam, but you've only been gone a few hours," she replied. "Did something happen down at the old churchyard? Is everything okay?"

"Everything's fine, Mrs. Long," said Del.

"Ya, mom," Sam repeated. "Everything's fine. Where's dad?"

Sam's mother released her son and went over and gave Del a hug as well. This was not unusual as she and Sam's father always treated Del like one of the family. Del knew she was always welcome at their house. It felt good to be hugged by Sam's mom, but it made Del long even more for this kind of genuine affection from her own mother. She saw the way Sam's family interacted and wanted that for herself. She wanted a mom and a dad who were normal and caring. She was sure that, when she finally went home, she would get a hug from her own mother, but it wouldn't be at all the way Sam's mom hugged him.

"Good to see you Del," said Mrs. Long, releasing her grip from Del. "Sam, your dad is out grocery shopping, so there isn't much here to eat. But there is some iced tea made in the fridge if you two want some. I have to go tend to the garden a bit."

"Okay," said the children together as Mrs. Long left by the back door.

Sam grabbed the jug of iced tea from the fridge and poured two tall glasses. The pair took up places on stools at the island where they had sat hundreds of times before. Del loved the times alone with her best friend, away from the other boys. These were always the times where Sam shone: where his intelligence, wit and humour would come through. He wasted no time in getting right to the point.

"I believe you, Del," he said.

"What?"

"I believe you," he said again.

"What do you mean, you believe me? About which part?" Del was a little taken aback.

"All of it. I don't think you made any of it up, and I don't think whatever you were sick with would make you mistake a dream for reality. I believe all of it. Crimson, Blythe Thicket, everything."

Del just sat there for a moment, then said, "Why didn't you say anything in front of Phil and Guy?"

"Phil and Guy loved the Mr. Thicket they knew," Sam replied. "So they just can't believe he's evil. They loved him from the moment that he jumped off his bird and saved us. I think you and I were suspicious of him from the beginning, so it's easier for us to see him as the heir of Mordlum. It's easier for us to see that he was lying to us."

Del admired Sam's ability to understand people. She just wished he would speak up more when others were around.

"So, what are you saying?" Del asked.

"I'm saying we should go back," said Sam. "You and me. I can't tomorrow, but Monday we should go."

"Are you serious?" Del said.

"Ya," said Sam. "I know you, Del. You're not going to let this go. You're going to go back, and if I don't go with you, you'll probably try to go alone."

Sam was right. The thought of returning to Azdia alone had already crossed Del's mind.

"It's the first day of school on Monday," Del said. "But we could just head to the church right after school. Do you think we should try one more time with Phil and Guy?"

Del pulled out her phone, thinking she should text them.

"Why don't we wait until Monday and see," Sam said, as he stopped her hand with his.

Del nodded in agreement, then said, "Sam?"

Their hands were still touching, and Del looked directly into his eyes.

"Yes?" Sam said expectantly.

"There's a new riddle," she said.

"No way!" Sam said. "Okay, you've got to tell me. But first, I propose a toast."

Sam and Del lifted their glasses of iced tea high in the air and proclaimed loudly, "To Mr. Thicket!"

Thank you for joining Del, Sam, Phil, and Guy in Azdia.

Enjoyed the story?
Here's what you can do next.
If you loved the story and have a moment to spare, I would really appreciate a review.

Reviews Make a Huge Difference
Most readers never leave reviews, but they make a massive difference. Reviews help other readers find good books by helping books like this become more visible. Unless you happen to have a following of thousands, the best place to leave a review is on Amazon. Search for the book there and you can give a rating and leave a few, hopefully kind, words.

Has anyone ever recommended a book to you?
I bet they have. Who can you recommend this book to? Who might love Del Ryder and the Crystal Seed. Tell them about it. Better yet, lend this book to them. Better still, buy them a copy.

SIGN UP FOR MY EMAIL NEWSLETTER

You can get the latest news about upcoming novels by visiting mattbrough.com and signing up for my email newsletter.

You will also get inside looks into where I am at in the writing, editing and production process as well as some insight into future projects, and maybe even some free stuff (when I have free stuff available)!

I don't send constant updates and won't fill up your inbox, so feel free to sign up today.

mattbrough.com

AUTHOR'S NOTE

When I set out to write Del Ryder the Crystal Seed, it was few weeks before my daughter's fifth birthday. I hoped I would have it completed by the time my daughter was ten years old. The story was completed in just a few months, several months before she would start kindergarten. At the time of writing this note she is just beginning to read and sound out a few words like "cat" or "bat." I guess I will need to wait for her to read this novel and I will have to be satisfied with other children and adults enjoying Azdia, its inhabitants, and its visitors.

I therefore cannot be more thankful to you, reader, for spending time with this novel. It is my first novel, after having many stories and book ideas, mostly non-fiction, bounce around in my head and leak out, sometimes in drips and drabs. This is the first book that has "stuck" and I'm glad to now be committed to writing several books in the Del Ryder Series. It was a delightful story to create and I'm looking forward to the future instalments. I hope you are too.

ACKNOWLEDGMENTS

Before a grand thank you list must come an acknowledgement of God's overwhelming grace. It may be cliche to thank God in acceptance speeches and the like, but I wish to do it anyway. I am most thankful to God for sabbath, for times of rest. It is liberating to know that the world will keep going with or without me, so if I took some time to write a book, the sky would not fall. I attribute any inspiration that may have crept its way into these pages to God's wonderful creativity.

There are also a number of people I would like to thank. My wife, Cheryl, has been a constant source of encouragement. She helped me work out the ending to this novel while we ate a steak dinner one night at the Keg. She was also the first to read an early draft of this book and gave excellent early notes, and continued reading drafts and giving feedback throughout the editing process. Thank you to my daughter, Juliet, who patiently let me talk about "daddy's book" at the supper table.

Thank you to all my family and friends who supported me. To my surprise when I told people I was writing this book, everyone was supportive, so that list is far too long to put here and risk that someone will be left out. I do wish to mention the following people who gave meticulous notes on early drafts: my mother, Ann, my aunt, Christine, and my sister, Tracey. Thank you as well to my final draft proofreaders: Mary, Sheila, Erin, Suzanne, and Paul. I could not have gotten this book done without support from a few friends and family members who encouraged me along the way in big and small ways: my dad, David, Kirsten, Conrad, Rebecca, Sarah, Stewart, Nikita, Izac, Sue, Liza, Matt, Jen. Thank you each one.

ABOUT THE AUTHOR

Matthew David Brough lives in Winnipeg, Manitoba in Canada with his wife Cheryl and their daughter Juliet. He is the author of the Del Ryder series, blogs at mattbrough.com, and is also the pastor of Prairie Presbyterian Church. Not surprisingly, some Christian themes, such as grace, forgiveness, healing, sacrifice, and community, tend to show up in the pages from time to time.

Matthew is strongly influenced by the classics: Shakespeare, J.R.R. Tolkein, C.S. Lewis, and of course, Star Wars.

Follow Matthew on twitter: twitter.com/mbrough

Or email Matthew at matt@mattbrough.com

CPSIA information can be obtained at www.ICGtesting.com
Printed in the USA
LVOW06s0900220815

451157LV00001B/26/P